Calico Captive

Calico Captive

ELIZABETH GEORGE SPEARE

Illustrated by W. T. Mars

HOUGHTON MIFFLIN COMPANY

To MARY

FOREWORD

In August, 1754, on the brink of the French and Indian War, James Johnson, his wife Susanna, and their children were captured in an Indian raid on Charlestown, New Hampshire. They were taken from their home, forced to march through the wilderness to the north, and sold to the French in Montreal, where they were held for ransom. Years later, when she was nearly seventy years old, Susanna Johnson wrote an account of this journey, and it is from her narrative that the main events of this story are taken.

Captured with Susanna and her family was a younger sister, Miriam Willard. Her imagined adventures, as they might have happened, are recounted here.

Calico Captive

CHAPTER I

PHINEAS WHITNEY was the last guest
to leave the party. Miriam Willard had been aware,
watching from the corner of her eye, of how he had
maneuvered to be the last one out the door. The
others were already out of sight down the dark path,
keeping close together, their laughter and boisterous
spirits stilled. The women hurried nervously beside
the silent men who kept to the outside of the path,
muskets ready at hand, for of late the Indians lurked
very close to the settlement. But Phineas seemed in
no hurry to join them. He stood just inside the warm
lighted cabin, leaning easily against the heavy doorpost, as though the evening were just beginning. The
crest of his short fair hair, bleached by the summer
sun, reached a good four inches above the lintel log,
so that he would have to duck his head to go through
the door. Miriam, who was going to be small like all
the Willard women, had to tip her head back to look
at him.

" 'Twas a very fine party," he said. "I had no idea
that New Hampshire would be such a gay place."

1

Miriam's gray eyes widened. Could he be serious? "You can't judge by tonight," she protested. "Could you have seen us this summer you wouldn't have found us very gay."

"Are you sure it is not always a holiday here?" he persisted, as though he had not had plenty of chance to observe, in the past few days, the endless struggle it took just to survive in this northern settlement. "Watching you tonight, I should have thought you spent every evening dancing the reel."

Had that been true she would know better how to answer him, Miriam thought. She wished she had some easy bantering words like his own; but what chance had she ever had, here in the wilderness, to practice such words?

"To tell the truth," she admitted instead, " 'tis the very first party I've ever been to. Once when the saw-mill went up they danced on the new boards, but I was too young to be allowed."

"Then I'm thankful I came in time for your first party," said Phineas, dropping his teasing. "And 'twas the first I've been to for a long time. My family doesn't hold much with dancing. Besides, I've been away from home for two months. You can't guess what it means, after tramping through the woods for so long, to find such friendly folks. It is going to be hard for me to leave this place."

2

Miriam had always said straight out whatever came into her head, and the question was out now, before she could think better of it.

"Must you leave soon?" she asked him, and then gave herself away still further by a scarlet blush.

"I have to enter Harvard College in a few weeks," he answered. "I am going to study for the ministry. And with the war starting up again, travel is uncer-

tain, and there may be delays on the way back. That is why I have to speak more urgently to you than I should. We have so few days left to get acquainted, Miriam. Will you think less of me if I make the most of them?"

No one had ever spoken to her like that before, nor looked at her as this young man was looking — so intently that she was not sure how her voice would sound if she tried to answer. Finally she grasped at a safe topic.

"I've heard about Harvard College. It must be a very grand place."

"Oh no, not grand at all. 'Tis a place for working and studying very hard. I visited there once. I'll tell you about it — if I may stay a little?"

Miriam looked back over her shoulder, but her sister and brother-in-law gave her no encouragement at all. Susanna, pretending not to notice the pair in the doorway, was already snuffing out the candles, scraping wax from the oak table where it had overflowed the saucer, and James stood in the middle of the room giving way to a great yawn. Phineas could scarcely miss such a hint.

"What must they think of me?" he said with chagrin. "I know it is far too late. After all, there is tomorrow, isn't there?"

"Of course there's tomorrow," Miriam smiled. "And

I'm sure Susanna will invite you for supper. Now see if you can catch up with the others, Phineas. 'Tis not wise to walk far by yourself."

Still he lingered, lowering his voice so that only her ears could hear. "Do you realize," he asked, "that tomorrow morning will be the fifteenth time I have seen you? That first day you were standing inside the gate as we came in. The second time was when you brought the lunch to your brother in the clearing."

So he had noticed even then! Miriam kept her eyes on the line where the edge of her blue dress hid the crack on the floor. It was on the tip of her tongue to say that all of those fifteen meetings had not been by accident. She had been hard put to it to find excuses for so many trips to the fort. But Phineas hurried on, saving her from such an unseemly confession.

"There I go," he checked himself, mistaking her silence. "There'll be a better time to say such things. But not time enough. When I think how it was the smallest chance that brought me to Charlestown!"

Chance? Or was it something more than chance, this meeting? The question trembled in the air as plain as though one of them had spoken it. Suddenly the moment was too full.

"I am really going now," he determined, swinging open the door. But his steady blue gaze went on speaking so unmistakably that Miriam had to look away.

"You must hurry," she whispered, both regretful and relieved, "or they will have barred the gate."

She bolted the heavy log door securely behind him as he strode off down the path. Then she turned impatiently back to the room. How could they be sleepy? She herself was wide awake to her very toes, though it was well past midnight and she had been up before dawn, sewing when she could scarcely see the needle. She could have danced right through till morning. The air about her still seemed to vibrate with the twang of the fiddle and stamp of boots on the board floor.

For all her busyness with the candles, Susanna had not missed a detail. "So," she observed now, "we're to have company for supper tomorrow?"

Miriam was in a mood to ignore both the sharpness and the curiosity that shone in her sister's eyes. "You don't mind, do you Susanna?" she coaxed. "Oh, it was such a wonderful party! When can we have another?" Her hoopskirt swayed as her feet tapped out a soundless measure.

"If you want another party," Susanna snapped, tart from sleepiness, "you can help a little next time instead of sitting in a corner sewing a dress all day long." But she softened as she looked again at her sister, at the vivid young face, the shining gray eyes, the slim figure in the flowered calico.

6

"I guess it was worth it, at that," she admitted. "The dress is lovely, though 'tis a wonder some of that basting held, the way you were swinging through the reel. You do have a knack for sewing, Miriam."

"I will help next time," Miriam promised quickly. "But I couldn't go to my first party in that old brown homespun." She smoothed the skirt of the new dress, marveling at the way the clear blue had turned to a soft gray in the dim light from the embers. She did have a knack. Her grandmother had taught her to cut and match, to take tiny even stitches. But no one had taught her how to mold the bodice snugly around her tiny waist, or how to gather the skirt so that it swirled just so about her ankles. "Besides, if it hadn't been for the dress — " She couldn't finish the sentence.

Susanna laughed, seeing the pink come up in her cheeks. "I know. The young man from Boston might not have noticed. Looks like you've got yourself a beau, Miriam. Do you think I didn't see how his eyes followed you every move you made?"

James laughed sleepily, and reached out a long arm to give Miriam's chestnut curls a playful tug.

"What's happened to our little sister?" he asked. "Two months ago you were just a little redheaded tomboy. Seems hardly fair to fool a young fellow like that."

"She's as old as I was when you met me," Susanna

reminded him, "and 'tis high time she had a little fun. It has been a dull summer for her."

"Be thankful 'twas dull," said James. "Could have been worse." His eyes were gentle as he looked at his wife. In another month her fourth baby would be born, and although she had not complained, the strain of the summer had put dark smudges under her eyes and an unaccustomed edge to her voice. Tonight she had been more like her old self, enlivening with her merry wit the sober faces of her guests, filling their cups with flip, or sitting contentedly against the wall watching the twirling couples.

"It is almost over," James reminded her now. "In a few weeks we will be back in Massachusetts. Have you told Miriam that she is coming with us?"

Miriam stared from one to the other. "Me? You mean you'll take me with you — to stay?"

"Do you want to go, Miriam?" asked Susanna. "Or would you rather stay here at Number Four and keep house for Father?"

Miriam's brightness clouded over. "Does Father want me to stay?"

"He says not, though he's like to be lonely when we've gone. Anyway, he may have to march off with the forces any day, and you shouldn't be here alone. You need more young ones your own age, and you can help the girls with their reading while Sylvanus is at school."

Miriam flung her arms rapturously around her sister. "Oh, Susanna, if you knew how I've hoped you would take me! I hate Number Four! I never want to see that fort again. 'Tis too good to be true. No dreadful Indians screeching in the night! And other girls to talk to!"

"And so much nearer to Boston!" finished Susanna. "Go to bed now, Miriam. 'Tis almost morning, and think of all the work we have to do."

"I don't want to go to bed," cried Miriam, twirling across the cabin, the blue calico flying out around her. "I'm so excited I can't possibly sleep. Everything is so wonderful all of a sudden. In just one day, how could everything have changed so much?"

But Susanna and James had talked long enough. There was nothing to do but climb the ladder into the loft, where the three children, four-year-old Susanna, two-year-old Polly, and six-year-old Sylvanus, slept soundly. They had stayed up hours past their bedtime, dancing and clapping their hands till they had collapsed on the bench against their mother's shoulder and been carried up the ladder and tucked into bed. Now they did not even stir as Miriam pulled the new dress over her head and hung it on a nail where she could see it the moment she waked. There was no leftover party warmth up here. Even in the August night she shivered. Pulling off the ruffled petticoat and stepping out of the hoops, she crawled in beside

9

little Susanna, and drew up the quilt against the damp chill.

But her thoughts could not be tucked in to sleep. Miraculously, as she had said to Susanna, the whole world had changed in just a few days. So much had happened, when for such an endless time nothing had happened at all.

A dull summer, her sister had said. How could James Johnson, adventuring off down the Connecticut River, have any idea what a summer it had been, that year of 1754, for the women left behind at the fort? After four years of uneasy peace, the Indians were again bent on war, stirred up by the French in Canada; and this struggling little community of Number Four at Charlestown, farthest north of the settlements along the Connecticut, was almost unprotected. The families whose men had gone trading had been forced to abandon their farms and move back into the shelter of the stout walls of the fort.

Day after endless hot day they had been crowded into those stuffy cabins with the whining children. The scanty grass inside the enclosure had shriveled and browned. The boys kicked up great curls of choking dust with their incessant scuffling. Outside the sky had shone a deep perfect blue. The children had peered through the timbers of the wall at fields that shimmered in golden sunshine, and woods that beckoned green and cool. But even at midday the women had seldom dared to venture more than a few feet from the palisade. In the night they had lain rigid in their bunks, holding their breath in the smothering blackness, hearing in the distance the blood-chilling Indian yells. Her sister Susanna had gone about abstracted, lips pressed tight, trying to find work enough to fill her days, always looking for excuses to go to the gate and search the road for a sign of her husband.

At last the men had returned, looking brown and hearty and full of high spirits at their successful trading. James Johnson had brought good news too. As soon as the summer crops were harvested, when the weather began to cool, he would take his family away from Number Four, with its hourly menace from the Indians. Susanna would have her baby in safety, in the cozy settlement of Northfield, Massachusetts. Miriam had not dared to mention her longing that they might take her too.

The day after the return, emboldened by James's musket, the Johnson family had left the protecting palisade and gone out to take possession of their own house again, a hundred rods distant. The children were wild with joy, running free and rolling in the long grass. Little Susanna had filled her arms with goldenrod, running to thrust it into Miriam's hands and darting back for more. Sylvanus had played he was an

Indian, sneaking from tree to tree, his sturdy little body plainly visible, popping out at them from behind bushes with shrill whoops. They had found the cabin untouched, musty from being boarded shut, and in the yard, overflowing with lush melon vines, plump grayish balls lay thick as hailstones on the ground. James had slit one open with his knife, and the juicy golden center lay like sunshine between his hands.

"Let's have a party!" Susanna had cried. "There are enough melons for a feast!"

"A party?" James had doubted. "With all the work that has to be done?"

"The work will be done," his wife had promised. "Right now is the time to celebrate your homecoming, and to entertain the visitors too."

One of the visitors was a tall young man, Phineas Whitney from Massachusetts, who had run across Captain Johnson's party and come along with them to visit this farthest outpost. To be honest, was it really leaving the fort, or the party, or even the prospect of Massachusetts that made the world seem so different? Or was it just this boy, with sun-lightened hair and blue eyes? Truly, it had not been the work, or the stifling summer inside the fort, or even the constant fear of Indians that had weighed on Miriam's spirit. It had been the loneliness. Of course she loved Susanna, just ten years older than she, who had been

12

both mother and sister, and she adored the children; but she longed for friends, for just one friend of her own. She had never known a girl her own age. She had never had a beau. Of the few young men and boys at the fort, now that she was too old for racing and climbing trees with them, she felt both shy and critical.

She had had so little experience. She could not have put into words just what sort of person she waited for. Yet from the first moment that Phineas had walked into the enclosure with the men, something within her had unmistakably recognized him. He was different from the men she had known. He was strong and practical as any of them, as he proved by setting to work straightway felling trees and dragging logs to repair the blockhouse. Inside of a half day the settlement had accepted him as though he had been born at Number Four. But there was a gentleness in his speech, and a purpose in his serious young face that set him slightly apart.

It was incredible, even though he had said it in his own words, that he had noticed her in the brown homespun, even before he had seen her in the blue dress. In her own mind the bolt of blue cloth that James had brought in his pack had changed her into a different person. The dress that hung close to her head, waiting for the first rays of the sun to light it into

13

beauty, symbolized the wonder of the past few days.

I'll have to put on the old brown dress in the morning, probably even for supper, she thought ruefully. But I can wear the blue to meeting on Sunday. And perhaps, if I do all the work, Susanna will have another party before Phineas goes. Oh, how can I lie still all the hours till sunup? I can never sleep a wink!

But she was sound asleep when the cabin shook with the tremendous knocking at the door.

THE KNOCKING startled Miriam wide awake. Pulling herself up to her knees, she knelt and peered down the loft hole. In the pale light she could see her brother-in-law James struggling into his jacket as he lurched, still half asleep, across the cabin floor.

"Confound you, Labaree," he muttered. "Do you have to be as early as all this?" He drew back the bolt and swung open the door.

Neighbor Labaree's solid figure filled the doorway, and his hearty voice boomed through the cabin. "Still abed, all of you? Thought you aimed to start on the south field before daybreak."

Without warning it happened. James Johnson's answer was drowned in such dreadful shrieks that Miriam's whole body turned to stone. She had heard them before, but far away, in the depths of the forest. Now they were close, close upon them. Indians! Labaree was jerked backward and the doorway was filled with bodies, pouring into the cabin with horrible yells. The half-light was a confusion of feathers, hideous faces streaked with red and white, tomahawks flashing. James leaped toward his musket, but three Indians were upon him in a flash, binding his arms tight against his body. Other redskins swarmed about the cabin, tearing open cupboards and chests, pawing over food and clothes, stuffing sacks with everything they could lay hands on. One slit open a feather bed, shaking out a choking cloud of feathers, and used the ticking as a bag to hold his plunder. Two of the savages came from the bedroom, dragging a shrinking and almost naked Susanna between them.

Terror suddenly stabbed Miriam's paralyzed mind and body into action. In a moment they would discover the loft stairs! The girl's wits came back to her. Behind her was a window, hardly more than a slit in the wall, but big enough, if she had to, to crawl through and escape. It was not too much of a drop to the ground. If she could get out, make a run for the fort, they might not notice. She could run as fast as any Indian. Once out of the cabin, her chances were good even in the woods. If she could reach the fort she could rouse the men and get help.

On hands and knees she crawled to the window and knocked out the shutter. In the din downstairs the clatter could not be heard. One bare leg was out and over the sill when her eyes caught a sight that stopped and held her. The children! They were wide awake, sitting up in their beds and watching her, without a sound, just looking, their eyes round and glassy like the eyes of little animals in the traps. Even at that moment Sylvanus struggled out of his covers and came scrambling toward her, whimpering like a frightened puppy.

A wave of anger swept over Miriam. "No!" she scolded. "No, Vanus! Go back!" But his small hands reached her and clung. Of a sudden she hated him, hated all three of them with their white faces. But for them she would be halfway to the fort by now. She dragged her leg back over the sill. She could not leave them.

"I'll let you down, Vanus," she whispered. "You run for the fort. Run as hard as you can! Sue, quick! Move, Sue! You go right after him!"

It was too late. An iron arm hooked round her waist and jerked her back. A brown hand reached round her and dragged Sylvanus away from the window. When she tried to struggle, a cruel twist of her wrist sent a stab of agony up to her shoulder. Half off her feet, she stumbled and fell after her captor, down the ladder, across the cabin floor, into the clearing outside.

The others were all there, even Peter Labaree, bound fast like James. The three children threw themselves sobbing against their mother, and Susanna, her

17

arms held by her two captors, tried to comfort them with her voice. "Hush, chickens," she faltered. "You're all to rights. Don't cry."

The Indians were arguing with each other in rough tones and menacing gestures. A few were bent on killing the prisoners at once, and their threatening tomahawks turned Miriam cold. Then one warrior, apparently the leader, stepped forward and silenced the jabbering with one curt syllable. His eyes swept over the prisoners, scowling disdainfully at the women in their night shifts. He gestured to one of his men and barked a command. The Indian glowered, but he opened a sack stuffed to bursting with goods from the cabin, grudgingly pulled out three dresses, and threw them on the ground in front of Susanna.

A ruffled length of petticoat trailed from the sack. "That too?" Susanna pleaded, pointing. But if the Indian understood, he intended to part with nothing else. Susanna's arms were freed for a moment, and she picked up one of the dresses and drew it clumsily over her head. Miriam was tossed another, a gray homespun, worn and patched. Little Susanna, bundled into the third, was helpless to move, and when the Indian who had parted with it saw that the blouse of her mother's dress reached almost to the child's knees, he slashed at the cloth with his knife, ignoring her screech of terror, yanked the skirt away and stuffed

18

it back into his sack. Sylvanus was allowed a little jacket of his own. In this flimsy clothing they seemed to satisfy the Indians. With a horrid yell, the captors pushed, prodded, and dragged their prisoners into the woods.

Sharp cramps began to shoot up and down Miriam's arm as the iron fingers of her captor never lost their grip. They had turned away from the clearing straight

into the thicket where the thorns tore at her legs and stabbed her bare feet. The Indians were in a hurry now, sensing that the fort must have been aroused by the racket, and they forced their prisoners on impatiently. Poor Susanna, heavy with her unborn child, could barely keep pace. When one shoe caught on a root, the Indians jerked her forward without it, so that she limped awkwardly. Miriam, lost in her own misery, did not even notice her sister's plight.

I could have made it. Her thoughts went round and round. I had a chance. I might even have reached the fort but for that stupid Vanus. Actually, she knew that even if she could have saved herself she couldn't have helped the others. The men in the fort would not have dared to follow. Everyone knew that pursuit meant instant death for prisoners. She might have been safe herself, though, this very moment, inside those walls she had hated, which now seemed so precious a shelter. She had only her own softheartedness to thank that instead she was floundering through the brush at the mercy of these savages. Glancing up at their paint-streaked faces, Miriam could see no signs at all of any mercy.

When the sun was directly overhead they came to a halt. The children had made the three miles or so with less difficulty than the grownups. The two little girls, after several tumbles, had been slung across the redskins' shoulders like the sacks of goods. Sylvanus, with his sturdy little legs, had trudged alongside his captor, snuffling and wiping his tears against his jacket sleeve, but seemed none the worse for it. The Indians were fast losing patience with Susanna, who was quite plainly unable to go another step. They stood looking down at her sagging figure with such disgust that for an instant Miriam forgot her own fear in a stab of terror for her sister's life.

At a curt order from the leader, one of the Indians fumbled through a bag of the stolen supplies and produced a loaf of bread and a few apples and raisins. Divided among so many it made scanty fare, but even these few mouthfuls Miriam found hard to swallow.

"Better eat," advised Peter Labaree, who was nearest her.

"I'm not hungry," said Miriam. "What are they going to do with us, Peter?"

"If they're feeding us, that's a good sign. Means they don't mean to kill us. Not yet anyway."

The leader struck his tomahawk against a log meaningfully. "No talk!" he ordered. "We go now. Walk fast. No talk any!"

As they struggled to their feet again, Miriam saw that the Indians' keen ears had caught a sound, and that they were watching intently the little clearing along the river, their hands ready on guns and tomahawks. Then she heard it too, a snapping of twigs and a heavy footstep. Hope leaped up and died away. It was only Scoggins, the ancient, sway-backed horse of Mr. Stevens, grazing innocently along the river. Poor old Scoggins, always good for a joke at the fort, all at once seemed almost beautiful. One of the Indians raised his rifle, but the leader spoke again sharply. With a quick move, he stepped forward and unfastened the thongs that bound James Johnson's arms.

"Get horse," he ordered, pointing at Scoggins. "Get horse for squaw."

James, his arms free, gave one desperate look about the group, and Miriam knew what was in his mind. At once, however, James knew that his only hope lay in obeying the Indian's command, and he walked quietly toward the unsuspecting animal, holding in his hand the bit of apple that had been his share. Old Scoggins walked amiably into the trap, and in a moment had said goodbye to his peaceful river existence. Pilfered sacks and blankets were thrown over his back, and James hoisted his wife's limp weight into this improvised saddle.

The afternoon march seemed endless. The Indians were still in a hurry, eager to get as far as possible from the fort before night fell. Toward sunset they came out on the shore of the river, and the prisoners understood that they were to cross. They were given a short chance to rest while the Indians dragged together dry branches to make a raft. Then Susanna was pushed onto the raft, James Johnson was ordered to swim alongside, and Peter Labaree was given poor Scoggins to force to the opposite shore. Miriam, sitting with the children, watched the frail platform that held her sister waver and sway, but it reached the other side, and presently returned for her and the little girls. When they were all across, the Indians kindled a fire and hung over it the familiar copper kettles in which Miriam and Susanna had stirred so many meals in the snug safety of their own cabin. These they filled with stolen porridge.

As they waited for the porridge to boil, Miriam looked about at her captors. By some unspoken agreement, each one of the prisoners seemed to belong to the Indian who had first laid hands upon him. The Indian who had found Miriam in the loft was never far from her side, even now that he seemed to think it safe to let go of her arm. There were not so many Indians, only eleven in all, though they had seemed such a savage horde inside the cabin. Taking advantage of this moment's pause they were busily pawing over the goods they had plundered, now and then letting out cackles of delight as something struck their fancy. Miriam saw a candlestick and two of

Susanna's silver spoons, and then with a stab of real anguish, she caught a glimpse of blue flowered calico. The new dress! The Indian who was in the act of yanking the precious goods out of his sack looked up and caught her longing gaze, and a taunting grin broke over his dark features.

Why, he's young, Miriam realized with a shock. Much younger than the others. And he's laughing at me. He knows it's my dress. Helpless fury surged hotly over her. I hate him! she raged inwardly. I could kill him for touching my dress with his dirty fingers.

Following another guttural argument, the Indians decided to pitch camp in this place, very evidently blaming Susanna for slowing them up. After standing and looking at her for a long moment, the leader shrugged and left her alone, whether from scorn or pity it was hard to tell. Certainly she would not try to escape, but precautions had to be taken with the others. The Indians split branches and fashioned a crude sort of stocks over the legs of the men, tied by thongs that fastened high overhead on limbs of trees. The children fared better. Sue and little Polly had their ankles tied, but were given blankets. To her horror, Miriam was forced to lie down between two Indians, a heavy cord thrown over her body and held securely under theirs. All this was done in silence. The Indians spoke few words, and any attempt to speak on the part of the prisoners was met with fierce threats.

Long after the Indians were asleep, Miriam lay rigid with mortification and fury between the two guards. They were so close that every breath she drew was filled with the heavy bear-grease odor of their bodies. They had taken no pains to choose a smooth sleeping place. Twigs poked her back, and a sharp pebble bit into one shoulder. She could not roll over, and she dared not even ease her aching muscles for fear the slightest tug on the cord would waken them. With the darkness a new torment had commenced; the air was swarming with mosquitoes, whining and biting savagely. More than that, now that the shock of their captivity was wearing off, she had time to be afraid. Where were they going? What did the Indians have in store for them? All her life Miriam had heard tales of white men taken captive by Indians, some stories so horrible that the older settlers' voices would sink to whispers if a child were around. Those whispers, the fearful looks, the terrible words she had been able to catch, tortured her now. If she could only speak to Susanna, even to Labaree or James, they might be able to give her a little comfort.

Sharper than hunger and fear, the memory of the blue dress pricked her. At the thought of its lovely folds crumpled in that hateful boy's hands, the tears

25

flooded her eyes, and turning her head against the ground, Miriam let them fall. There in the wilderness, surrounded by savage enemies, bound for a fate she dared not imagine, she wept her heart out for a flowered dress she would never wear again.

CHAPTER 3

THEY WERE PUSHING forward next morn-
ing in a chill fog and drizzle when a new vexation was
added to Miriam's distress. She had begun to relax a
little, the watery gruel warm in her stomach and her
strong young body rested from a brief sleep. With the
war paint washed off their faces, the Indians looked
far less terrifying, and they had only troubled to bind
the two men, feeling sure of the women and children.
The whole party was walking single file now through a
dense wood where only the Indians could recognize a
trail. Miriam's captor walked ahead of her, and beyond him little Susanna rode quiescent on the shoulders of another redskin. Polly's captor was out of sight.
Curiously enough, the Indians had accepted the fact
that Polly, unlike the cowed Sue, was docile only so
long as she was in sight of her mother. The moment
the trees hid from her that familiar figure hunched
on the back of old Scoggins, no threats could subdue
her wails. The Indians had shown surprising patience
with this behavior, and the brave who carried Polly

27

waited stolidly in the trail whenever Susanna was forced to rest.

Farther ahead in the fog Sylvanus' eager voice now and then broke the silence. He had lost all fear of the Indians by now, and was not at all discouraged that his friendly prattle met a stony response. He seemed to sense that he could get away with more freedom than any of the others dared attempt.

All at once Miriam's dress caught on something, and she fell forward, scraping her hands. Looking back, she saw the hateful young Indian just behind her, and once again she caught a glitter of derision in his black eyes. Plainly he found her awkward stumble amusing. A few minutes later she tripped again, and this time she looked up just in time to see him spring back, grinning openly. The Indian ahead motioned her to her feet with an impatient gesture.

"He stepped on my dress," Miriam flared. "He tried to make me fall!"

Her master shrugged and moved forward. Her

cheeks hot, Miriam bunched her skirt into both hands and stumbled after him. With both hands full of skirt, however, there was no way to ward off the brambles and low-hanging branches that snapped back against her. Her captor gave no sign that he noticed, but presently he motioned her to stop, and whipping out his knife he neatly sliced a spiral of green vine that swung from a tree and handed it to her with a rough gesture toward her skirt. Miriam stared at him. Could this be a sign of thoughtfulness? Or was he merely impatient at her slow progress? She could read no slightest softening in that stern face. However it had happened, she accepted the vine gratefully and made a clumsy job of tying up her billowing skirt.

After that the walking was easier. But presently the boy behind her crept closer and gave a playful tug at her hair, a tug that hurt and sent stinging tears to her eyes. Miriam's temper mounted. Not one of the boys at the fort had ever tried to pull her hair twice. But here there was no way to retaliate.

He knows I can't do a thing about it, she thought angrily. But I know one way to spoil his fun. He's not going to have the satisfaction of seeing me blubber like Polly. Setting her lips tight, Miriam held her head higher than ever and set her feet straight ahead.

When soon afterward they caught up with the rest of the party at a clearing, Miriam was shocked out of her own vexation at the sight of her sister. Susanna had collapsed on the wet ground. Her face was hidden, but her shoulders moved in a rapid, shuddering breath, and now and then her whole body seemed to draw tense with anguish. Four Indians stood looking down at her with ugly scowls. Plainly another argument was beginning. Suddenly, to Miriam's horror, one of the Indians raised his tomahawk and brandished it over the woman's head. The whole terrified group of prisoners held their breath. But another warrior knocked the lifted arm aside. The two braves faced each other with angry shouts. Then the leader spoke, one curt word, and the two turned away sullenly.

At another command they set to hacking down fir branches, and with unbelievable speed they constructed a small shelter of green boughs. James Johnson, his arms unbound, bent over his wife, lifted her gently, and helped her to walk the few steps, holding the branches carefully aside till they were both hidden from view. The rest of the party, seeing that there would be a wait, settled down on the ground to rest. The children simply dropped where they were and were almost instantly asleep.

Miriam edged closer to the man who rested against a tree trunk. "What is it, Peter?" she whispered. "Is Susanna very ill?"

30

"She is in labor," said Labaree soberly.

"In labor? You mean the *baby*? Peter! She can't be! A baby can't be born out here!"

"Babies have been born in all sorts of unlikely places," answered Labaree. "At any rate, your sister is going to need your help."

"My help!" Miriam was terrified. She shook her head violently. "I couldn't, Peter. She can't expect me to do that. I wouldn't know what to do."

Labaree said nothing, and Miriam stood staring at the leafy booth. This was an ordeal she had not counted on at all. Through her mind flashed a memory of the day Polly had been born. She remembered Annie Howe, who had borne nine children of her own, and had lost track of how many others she had helped into the world. She could see Annie now, bustling into the cabin, pink-faced and clean, smelling of good strong soap, poking up the fire, hustling the children outside with good-natured smacks, shaking with laughter at her own jokes, making it all seem easy and matter of fact and good. But here in this chill forbidding place there was no capable Annie to take charge, only a frightened girl with no knowledge at all.

Labaree's silence made her uncomfortable. More than Labaree, all of them seemed to be watching her, judging her for a coward. There was no sound from the shelter. How long would it be? Suddenly Miriam

31

knew that no matter how she dreaded to go in, she could not bear to wait outside another moment. She was a white girl; her place was with Susanna, not out here with these savages. Running across to the shelter, she stooped down and crawled inside.

Susanna, lying on a pile of fir branches, turned her head weakly. "Oh Miriam," she breathed. "I'm so thankful you're here."

Miriam never forgot her sister's courage on that day. With the same stubbornness that had brought her parents into a wilderness to found a new home in spite of cold and hunger and unending labor, Susanna fought now to bring her child into the world. Two hours later Miriam held in her hands a baby girl, a perfect, tiny, red morsel, who opened her thin little button mouth in a pathetic wail.

As though someone outside had been waiting for that signal, there was a rustling of the green boughs, and an arm thrust inside a little pile of clothing. As James Johnson picked it up, Miriam was struck by the realization that the Indians had chosen the finest and softest of their stolen articles for the newcomer. Wrapping the tiny wrinkled body in a warm old hood of Polly's, she caught Susanna's eyes following her every move, and bent nearer to let Susanna see her child. It was almost impossible to believe, but there was happiness in the mother's eyes. Even here in this place she welcomed a new baby with love and pride.

"We will call her Captive," Susanna murmured. "Poor little one. What does she have to live for?"

James smoothed back the matted hair from his wife's face. "She is in God's hands, as we all are," he said gently. "He has been merciful enough to bring her to us safely. We must go on trusting Him. Now sleep, my dear. Sleep while you can."

"Take her outside, and let the children see," Susanna begged. "And then let her sleep here with me."

Outside the shelter Miriam noticed that the Indians were very curious and more than a little impressed. They followed with sharp glances but made no objection as James and Miriam walked over to the three children huddled together with awe-filled eyes, and showed them their new sister. One of the Indians brought Miriam a long wooden spoon to feed her with, and another, one of the two who had Susanna in charge, even came very close and poked his face into the tiny bundle and studied it curiously. Then he capered off like a silly schoolboy in delight. "Two monies!" he cackled, holding up two dark fingers. "Two monies for me!"

"The hateful thing!" Miriam blazed, watching him. "What does he mean, for him? What does he intend to do with the baby?"

"He thinks the baby will bring him double money,"

33

Peter Labaree spoke up. "We ought to be glad to hear it. It means he will take care to keep the little mite alive."

"True," agreed James. " 'Tis the best sign we've had so far. Though I suspected it when they allowed Susanna to live."

"Suspected what?" asked Miriam. "Why is it a good sign, James?"

"I believe they intend to sell us, instead of keeping us captive. The French are offering more money for live prisoners than for scalps. We've been moving steadily north. I reckon we'll come out somewhere along the border of Canada."

"You think they're not going to kill us? You really think that, James?"

"We're a lot more valuable alive," Peter Labaree agreed. "Provided we don't try their patience too far."

"We must do our best not to," said James. "If they will just give Susanna a little time to rest. Try and talk to the children if you can, Miriam. Tell them we must keep marching with good courage and do nothing to provoke them. I have great hope we may all come through this together."

Miriam felt her knees suddenly weak. For two days she had not dared to look ahead or to hope at all. The relief was almost more than she could bear. Peter Labaree saw her waver and held out his arms.

34

"You've done a fine day's work, girl," he told her. "Let me take the babe now. Never fear, I know what to do for her. I've three of my own."

Miriam surrendered little Captive with gratitude. She was so tired she longed to drop down on the wet pine needles and in sleep forget everything that had happened. For a while she had forgotten how hungry she was, and now the very thought of food made her faint. Suddenly she was struck by a sharp new fear.

"But James," she cried, "if they sell us to the French, won't we be slaves? They will own us, won't they?"

Slavery she had heard of, too. It was the most dreaded word known to these white men and women, who were not afraid of work or privation or hostile Indians so long as they knew themselves to be their own masters.

"Aye," admitted James. " 'Tis not too happy a prospect, but still the best we can hope for. Some I've known have found it not too hard. I believe the French are open to reason. They are usually willing to ransom their prisoners."

"Don't trouble yourself too much, Sister," he added kindly. "Sooner or later we will get word back to the fort. Give me the babe now, Peter. I fear my wife will not rest without her."

Peter Labaree looked down at little Captive cradled gently in his big arms. "She minds me of my youngest," he said. "Only three months ago I held her for the first time."

James Johnson laid a hand briefly on his friend's shoulder as he turned back to the shelter. Looking up at their muscular six-foot neighbor, Miriam saw that there were tears in his eyes.

CHAPTER 4

I CAN TALK Indian," Sylvanus boasted. "Want to hear me talk Indian, Miriam? *Nebi,* that means water."

"What do you want to talk Indian for, Vanus?" snapped Miriam. " 'Tis a horrid language."

"I don't think so. I can walk like an Indian too. See how Ahtuk walks? He makes his toes go like this."

"Vanus, you ought to be ashamed of yourself."

"Why? Ahtuk says I'm a *wskinnossis.* I'm going to be a big brave when I grow up."

"You are not. You're going to be a captain like your father, and don't you forget it. Vanus, what's got into you to be so friendly with the Indians? They're wicked. They're our enemies."

Sylvanus was only six years old. Miriam's ideas of loyalty were far too complicated to understand. To him this march through the wilderness was an exciting excursion after a summer cooped up in the fort. The Indians let him do pretty much as he pleased, and he could see nothing frightening about them. No one

37

was fussing at him to wash his face or to learn his letters. He admired the tall naked body of his Indian owner, sinewy and powerful, which looked far more like a captain's to him than the exhausted plodding figure of his father. Of the whole wretched party, Sylvanus alone was thoroughly enjoying himself. Once when they stopped to rest, the Indian boy, wearied of teasing Miriam, stripped a slender ash bough and fashioned a small-sized bow and some light arrows, and showed the child, over and over again, how to aim and snap the deerhide bowstring. His hands over the small white ones were gentle. Susanna, watching them, burst into tears, and Miriam could not hide her indignation.

"Can't you tell Vanus not to?" she stormed to James. "He *likes* the Indians. He's forgotten already what they've done to us. 'Tis — 'tis disloyal!"

"Vanus is only a child," James rebuked her. "He has been lucky that the Indians have taken a fancy to him instead of abusing him. An Indian friend isn't a bad thing to have, Miriam. Indians have a sense of loyalty too."

That philosophy was incomprehensible to Miriam. She could never feel anything but hatred for a redskin. She hated them more every day of this miserable journey. She hated their unfathomable black eyes, their expressionless language. She shrank away from the food they offered for fear her fingers might touch theirs. Most of all she hated the boy, Mehkoa, with his arrogant swagger.

She could not remember how many days they had been dragging along at this slow pace. The days blurred together like an endless nightmare. Six, perhaps, or seven. Sometimes the sun filtered through the trees or scorched her shoulders as they followed an open riverbank. Other days it rained fiercely, weighting down her hair, and almost sealing her eyelids shut. Some days there had been almost no food at all, and she could have cried like the little girls with hunger cramps. When the Indians brought down a hawk or a woodchuck the slim portions were carefully divided so that even the Indians never had anywhere near enough. Two days ago, at a camping place, they had found supplies left from a previous camp, a skin bag of bear grease hung from a limb of a tree, and a bag of flour. That night they had feasted on pudding with bear-grease sauce, and broth seasoned with snakeroot. After that there had been nothing at all, until yesterday when the Indians had decided to shoot old Scoggins. The very thought of that meal still made her retch, but she had eaten it, like all the others, because her hunger was beyond endurance.

With Scoggins gone, the Indians had fashioned a kind of woven litter in which James carried Susanna on his back, a sore burden for his waning strength, even though Susanna looked so frail and wasted a breath might have blown her away. That Susanna endured those days at all was incredible. Sometimes, when the whole party came to a halt and Miriam saw her sister slump to the ground, she was filled with frantic impatience.

She holds us all up, she would despair. James said they would not bother with us too much. Any minute they may get fed up with her and decide to kill us all. If we could just do something about Susanna! If we could go ahead and leave her to rest somewhere. Without her we could get where we're going. Anywhere, just out of these woods. Anywhere where there'd be some food. But then a glimpse of Susanna's white face would shame her. Susanna never made a sound or gave a word of complaint.

Sometimes, Miriam thought, the thing that exasperated her most was Susanna's patience. She herself had so little. The baby Captive, for example, had driven her almost to the end of her endurance. At first they had taken for granted that, being the only other woman, she would care for the baby and carry it. Captive wasn't heavy, but she was a constant burden. She cried on and on, piercingly, for the food that she could not have. The sips of gruel when they stopped to make a fire would quiet her for a few moments only. The crying rasped on Miriam's nerves until she could not bear it longer. Finally Peter Labaree had lifted the baby from her arms and taken charge. Certainly he had a way with babies, and there was far less wailing from that time on.

The moment she gave up Captive, the Indian boy was back at his tricks. She could not decide which was the worse torment, the bite-em-no-see-ems, as the Indians called the tiny black midges, or this unpredictable boy. Several times, surprisingly, he fell into step beside her, walking with the lithe grace of an animal, and attempted some conversation, which she scornfully rejected. Then he would fall behind her and devise some new trick for her discomfort. Though his irrepressible spirits occasionally provoked the older Indians to a snarl, he was obviously their favorite. Unless his pranks interfered with their progress they took no notice of him or of Miriam's embarrassment. Her one defense was her pride and a determination to do her best to spoil his pleasure. When a furry caterpillar dropped into her portion of gruel, or a small snake wriggled over her shoulder, she held her breath tight and did not even squeal. She wore her hair braided now like a squaw's, hanging forward over her shoulders, where he was less able to pull it. When a branch whipped back at her with cruel intention, she bit her lips and marched scornfully ahead.

41

It was a sort of game between them, a cruelly unfair game with all the odds on his side. But she was a white girl. This loathsome boy would not have the satisfaction of making her cry.

The seventh day was nearly over when Miriam suddenly remembered something. It was her birthday, and for the first time in all her life no one had remembered or wished her happiness. What a silly thing, to want someone to wish her happiness when heaven only knew what horrors were in store for her! This was the day when she had hoped for another party, when she would have danced again in the blue dress — with Phineas Whitney! Now the thought of him, which she had pushed back to the edges of her mind all this week, flowed over her with a great lonesome ache that was worse than hunger. Did he share even a little of this heartache? What had he felt that morning when he learned that their few days together had been lost? Tears gathered in her eyes and would surely have spilled over, except that just in time she caught the Indian boy's curious glance and winked them back.

The party ahead had come to a halt again on the shore of a small river, Otter Creek, Peter Labaree guessed. Miriam had learned to dread these brooks and rivers to be crossed. They meant slippery moss and sharp rocks hidden under wet leaves, and soggy clothes that never really dried out in the forest damp. This creek looked really frightening. The water rushed swiftly, and just below them it broke into rapids with a roar that echoed against the rocky banks and drowned out their voices. The Indians were evidently familiar with the creek, and were deliberately choosing a crossing place. They pointed, indicating a path from rock to rock.

"No step that way," the leader warned. "Big hole there. Very deep."

Two of the Indians were sent ahead to point out the route they were to follow. Then James Johnson, with the litter that held Susanna, stepped in carefully and forced himself into the current. Besides being swift, the creek was deeper than anything they had waded before, and Miriam's heart sank as she saw the water creeping up above the man's waist and closing over her sister's shoulders. Three Indians each swung a child to his shoulder. Polly, in terror as the cold water crept up her bare legs, caught her captor's black tuft of hair in both hands and clung desperately. Peter Labaree had to hold the baby Captive up over his shoulders to keep her blanket dry. The leader motioned Miriam to follow.

The sting of the icy water snatched away her breath. It took all her caution to keep a footing on the mossy stones, and the pull of the current terrified her. Ac-

43

tually, when it came to deep water she was as much a coward as Polly. At home in Charlestown some of the boys had learned to swim in the river, but for a girl, even for a tomboy, such a sport was forbidden. She must make sure that she did not fall.

She had just reached the deep water and braced herself against the pull of the current when a fearful thing happened. Labaree, just ahead of her, tottered, lost his footing, flung out one arm to save himself, and fell headlong into the creek, losing his grip on the precious bundle he carried. With a gasp of horror Miriam watched the dirty scrap of blanket that held the baby Captive whirling round and round like a leaf.

Then, without thinking, she plunged forward and struck out wildly. Her fingers touched the blanket and clutched it tightly in a spinning whirlpool. But her flailing feet could not find bottom again. She had gone off the course — into the deep hole the Indians had warned against. The current was too powerful to fight. It pushed her faster and faster, and the roaring was all around her like thunder.

Panic blocked out every thought. But somehow she kept her hold on the blanket. Suddenly her body hit against some object with a sickening jolt, and automatically her free arm grabbed hold. Gasping and choking, she clung fast, and when her eyes cleared she saw that she was flattened against a submerged

44

log caught against the rocks, its jagged tip jutting out of the rapids. Gasping for breath, Miriam struggled with her awkward bundle and managed to heave the baby up and to hold her propped against the log only a few inches above the rushing water.

Gradually her breath came back. As her own panic quieted, she felt a needle of fear for the baby. She could not turn her head or free a hand to move the blankets, nor hear a sound in this roaring, but presently she felt a slight jerking against her arm. The baby was kicking feebly, and a choking wail came thinly through the thunder, close against her ear. Captive was alive. If only she could manage to hold her up out of the water till help came. But the awkward position was back-breaking, with the other arm straining to hold them both to the wet log. Its rough bark scraped her ribs unbearably.

She could see the rest of the party on the bank and could watch their excited gestures, though she could not hear what they were trying to shout to her. She was only vaguely aware of what they were doing. She did not see the Indian searching his pack or remember the length of new rope James Johnson had brought back from his trading. She could not see the Indians recrossing the creek above her, or the stone that hurtled across the rapids over her head with a slithering length of rope attached. After what seemed an

45

endless length of time, however, she realized that something lay across the water, and as it gradually stretched taut she realized that it was a rope, only an arm's length away, from bank to bank. Almost within reach, but too far to be any good to her. She dared not let go the log. She knew she had not the strength to turn her body, to cling to Captive, to let herself into that swirling water again.

Then she saw that two Indians were coming out across the water, swinging easily and powerfully along the rope toward her — her own master and the young boy. Mehkoa reached her first. Holding out his arms for the baby, he tried to wrest Captive from her grasp. Miriam clung closer to the sodden blanket in terror.

She could not trust Mehkoa. Captive was safer with her, even here, than with that grinning savage.

"Give!" he shouted in her ear. "Give papoose. Mehkoa carry!"

With the swirling water about them, his dark eyes were very close to her own. There was no grin there now. He met her look honestly, and suddenly, with a sob, she gave the baby into his hands. At the same moment the other Indian reached her, and his hard arm went round her waist. The instant her grip on the log let go, Miriam lost consciousness.

When she opened her eyes, her first sensation was of blessed warmth. A roaring fire crackled within a foot of where she lay, sending a glow that penetrated the soggy rags that clung to her body. Then she felt warmth close to her face, and realized that James Johnson was holding the baby's wooden spoon against her lips. The first swallow of broth made a hot path deep inside. Raising her head, Miriam saw the others all around her, the silent Indians, the children, Susanna on her litter, and they were all watching her.

"Are you all to rights, Sister?" James asked. "We owe you much, more than we can say."

"I'm to rights," Miriam answered, pulling herself up. "The baby — is Captive safe?"

For answer, Susanna pulled aside the woolen jacket that had taken the place of the gray blanket. Captive's

47

wrinkled, red little face puckered up even more tightly at the disturbance, and her pitiful mouth opened in a hungry howl. Susanna raised her eyes and met Miriam's in a long grave look.

She knows, Miriam thought with wonder. She knows the dreadful things I have been thinking about her. And she knows that I will never think them again! Suddenly she was closer to her sister than ever before in their lives, and the love and courage shining from Susanna's eyes warmed her more deeply than the fire or the broth. Somehow, without a single word, their whole relationship was changed. Miriam had always been the little sister, always tagging along, always just a little at odds with the rest. Now she was a Willard too! For just one moment at least, Susanna's courage had been hers. She had measured up.

All at once, for the first time since that fearful morning in Charlestown, something like happiness bubbled up in her. Here she and Susanna both lay by the fire, soaked through and scarcely able to sit up, but Miriam felt that they stood side by side, and that whatever lay ahead the two Willard women would see it through together.

One of the Indians had shot and cooked a big bird of some kind, and now the steaming morsels were carefully divided. As her own master offered her a portion on a piece of bark, Miriam saw to her amazement that it was a piece of breast meat, the choicest bit. He offered it gravely, as though it were some sort of honor.

The meat was stringy and undercooked, but as she ate it slowly, making each bite last as long as possible, Miriam tried to sort out the bewildering ideas that had crowded upon her in the last few moments. What strange creatures these Indians were! Were those howling savages who had burst in upon them at Number Four the same men who had built a fire to dry their prisoners' clothes? Were those greedy barbarians, scrabbling for everything they could lay hands on, the same men who here in the forest scrupulously divided the meager food into equal portions and offered it to the prisoners before they had tasted it themselves? They were sly, ignorant animals, yet they had a sort of dignity about them.

They have treated us well, Miriam had to admit to herself. Nothing like those stories of what they do to prisoners. Yet I know they despise us, every one of us. If they don't abuse us, there is some reason in their minds, or perhaps they are too proud to bother with us. I can never understand them.

The real surprise, however, was still to come. After they had eaten, as the Indians prepared to march again, Mehkoa came toward her. She saw him coming, but she would not look at him, and turning her head away, she pretended to be absorbed in braiding her damp hair. She was aware that he stood waiting for a long time, but she would not look up. What if he had saved the baby? A baby meant only money to him. The Indians would not let any part of their prize slip through their fingers. She still hated him, and his devilish grin. Finally, however, her curiosity was too much for her, and she raised her head to look at him. He was holding something in his hands, something bright blue, and her heart leaped in unbelief. It was the blue dress!

"White girl wear," he said. "Old cloth no good any more. White girl put this on."

Miriam sat up and clutched the blue folds tight, as though they might be snatched away in one of his tricks. It would be like him. But he simply stood waiting for some word from her. Miriam turned her head away again. The dress was hers. He had stolen it, and he had no right to be thanked for it now. She wouldn't put it on either. She would carry it, every step of the way. Then, looking down, she saw that the boy was right; the old dress was no good. The rocks and the jagged log had torn the rotting fabric to shreds. She had no choice but to tramp through the forest in the only pretty dress she had ever owned. As the soft folds went over her head, Miriam felt her control suddenly cracking. She began to laugh, a laughter that sounded shocking and that she couldn't stop.

"Miriam, what is it?" James was instantly at her side. "Are you ill?"

"I got a birthday present," she sobbed. "Did you know it was my birthday? My only present, and it had to come from a horrid Indian. And 'tis too late to do me any good."

She hated Mehkoa more than ever. Yet somehow, she had a definite conviction that he would trouble her no further. It was only later, lying beside the fire, that it occurred to her to wonder, uncomfortably, if in the battle between her and the Indian boy it was she who had come out the winner after all.

CHAPTER 5

Miriam was long past caring that the precious dress was bleached and torn to a shapeless rag when at last the party reached the village of St. Francis. The prisoners had known for several days that a destination was near. They were traveling not on foot now, but in three Indian canoes. They had left the shining Lake Champlain behind, progressing by a series of rivers and streams, now wide, now narrow and swift. Twice they had stopped at French forts, once at Crown Point and once at Chamblec, and each time the French soldiers, though refusing to buy any prisoners, had handed out hot food and brandy. From these first encounters with the French, Miriam saw little reason to fear them. If it were Canada they were approaching, their fortunes were bound to improve.

The spirits of the Indians were visibly on the rise, and their pace was accelerated. Powerful bronze arms sent the three canoes racing with long rhythmic thrusts, and now and again shouts of unguarded triumph sent shivers down the spines of the prisoners cramped against the rough floors. By night, in the light of the fire they had built on the shore, the Indians danced, circling in an endless weaving chain around the fire, one brave after another breaking the pattern with violent, hideous contortions.

When they tired of dancing they rehearsed the prisoners for some future performance that must meet exacting standards. Each of the white prisoners was taught a special song. Over and over Miriam's master drilled her in the detestable, meaningless words, *Danna witchee natchepung.* Sylvanus was the only one who seemed to perform to the Indians' satisfaction. He would pose, legs astride, arms folded like a chieftain, and shrill *Narviscumption,* until they howled and slapped their legs with relish.

Finally, late one afternoon, the canoes drew up to a narrow strip of sand where the Indians donned war paint. Here for the first time each of the prisoners was daubed. Miriam held herself rigid as her master drew a bark twig across her cheeks and forehead, leaving a sticky smear of vermilion. Susanna looked like an apparition, her gaunt cheeks hideously spotted. Sylvanus was a comical little goblin, his baby face a striped replica of his master's.

"What is it for, Peter?" Miriam whispered, steadying the spoon against the baby's ravenous groping mouth, as they took advantage of the brief halt. "Are we coming to Canada?"

Peter Labaree rubbed his chin glumly. "No chance of that now," he said. "We've turned south again two days ago. Changed their minds, I mistrust."

"Then where are they taking us?"

"From the direction, I reckon Saint Francis."

St. Francis! The most dreaded word in all New England!

"Then they'll kill us!" she moaned, her fear breaking through the whisper. Peter lifted a warning hand.

"Steady now," he cautioned, taking the jerking spoon out of her fingers. "I think they're still bent on selling us to the French. Probably want to show us off first. And they need food as bad as we do."

"They burn people at the stake at Saint Francis!"

Labaree shook his head. "These Injuns are Abenakis. If they was Iroquois now, I wouldn't give much for our chances. With the Abenakis, I'd say the worst we've got to look forward to is the gantlet."

That was another of those words the women at the fort used to whisper. The gantlet — double lines of Indians armed with clubs and knives, through which a captive was lucky to come out alive.

"Keep your chin up, girl," advised Labaree, noting too late what his words had done. "You've got to allow these redskins have treated us decently enough so far."

They pushed on again, the Indians whooping and yelling in anticipation. Presently the tense nerves of the prisoners jumped to an answering clamor from the shore, as they swept toward a stretch of pebbly sand. Instantly, from the trees, a howling frenzy of women burst upon the shore. After the weeks of silence, the hubbub was paralyzing. Miriam shrank in the canoe and stared at the ragged screaming women, the naked shrill, excited children, and the dogs, countless mangy frantic creatures, leaping and yelping.

At a fierce gesture from her master she pulled herself up and cringingly stepped out on the shore. Surely she would be torn to pieces! But the leader was shouting above the uproar, and the women fell back. Booing and screeching with disappointment, they nevertheless obeyed, shoving the children, kicking the dogs, into a rough sort of line with an opening at the far end. Then, abruptly, there was silence. The gantlet! Even the children knew what it meant.

"Sing!" commanded the leader, pointing to Susanna.

55

Unbelievably, Susanna began to sing, a thread of a voice lifted quite clearly and steadily in the chant she had memorized. Clinging to James's arm, her head high, she moved between the lines of Indians, and not a single hand was raised against her. After her Polly and little Sue parroted their song and dance in terror and streaked past their mother to the other end.

"Sing!" ordered Miriam's master. "Sing! Dance fast!"

Under the grease paint, Miriam's face felt stiff. Her dry tongue could not make a sound. The snap of a switch stung her bare ankles, and her feet jerked involuntarily. The words came back to her, *Danna witchee natchepung!* Another stinging cut sent her scurrying after the others. A howl of derision greeted her undignified flight and, mortified, she halted beside her sister. Why couldn't she have carried it off like Susanna? Another roar, this time of approval, greeted Sylvanus, who was strutting as though he knew he bore a charmed life.

The gantlet was over. Labaree had been tripped, and blood trickled from an ugly bruise on his forehead, but not a hand had seriously been raised to harm any of them.

They had barely drawn a thankful breath when a deep throbbing drumbeat set them quivering afresh. In the center of the clearing stood a drum made of a tree trunk, as wide round as a washtub and high as a man's waist. The jabbering women were again stilled. The lines of the gantlet parted, and into the clearing between moved a row of warriors. Behind them strode a tall figure with towering shoulders under a scarlet blanket, his great beaked nose jutting beneath a tremendous feathered bonnet. His measured words fell like deeper drumbeats into the complete stillness.

Before this chief the prisoners were led, and each was solemnly considered. Susanna first was officially claimed by her master, who presented to her a belt of wampum, saluted her formally, and led her away, with Captive in her arms. Little Sue and Polly were claimed by squaws. When it came Miriam's turn, her master spoke at length to the Grand Sachem. For a long chilling moment the whole weight of that awful gaze held her motionless. Then he gave an order, and two women stepped forward. One was as shapeless as a bag tied through the middle, with brown wrinkled face, like a dried apple. The other was a girl, younger than Miriam, with a smooth copper skin and an unblinking stare of pure hatred.

These women led her away from the clearing, between a double row of squalid bark huts and wigwams, among which sagged an occasional decrepit log cabin. Her glance was caught by the hairy circles that dangled like flags from every doorpost, until with a prickle of horror she realized what they were — scalps! She turned away her eyes, and looked beyond the huts to a tottering church steeple with a huge cross black against the reddened sky. Then she blinked as she stepped through a doorway into the dimness of a wigwam.

There was a choking smell of wood smoke, of unwashed bodies, a fragrance of sweet grass, the redolence of boiling meat. A fire burned in the center of the wigwam, and nearby, on a pile of dirty blankets and skins, squatted a wizened and shrunken old woman.

The hasty pudding, ladled into a wooden bowl on the floor, sent up puffs of mouth-watering steam. The shapeless squaw handed her a wooden spoon, and after a moment's hesitation, Miriam sat clumsily down on the floor, to dip in her spoon with the others. A cackle like that of a hen in the barnyard broke from the toothlesss old squaw. With a flick of disdain in her black eyes, the Indian girl sank gracefully to her knees and back on her heels. Miriam flushed, aware of her own awkwardness, but at the first taste of the luscious dish she forgot her pride. She dipped the spoon again greedily, but after a few swallows her knotted stomach refused more food. She moved back dizzily, and while the others ate, she sat neglected on a ragged blanket, till the smells, and the strange jabbering, and the crackle of the fire blurred and wheeled into an exhausted sleep.

In the morning she was left to her own devices. The three Indian women busied themselves making moccasins. The woman, who said her name was Chogan, threaded colored beads and applied them expertly in a complicated design. The old grandmother smoothed and cut the soft skins, and the girl stitched the pieces together. After watching for a time while the women worked and chattered, Miriam ventured to the doorway and stood looking out, and as they still ignored her, she found courage to go in search of the others.

To her relief, Susanna called to her from a nearby doorway.

"How is it with you, Miriam?" she inquired anxiously. "Do they treat you well?"

"They don't pay me much attention," Miriam admitted. "Except for the girl. I think she'd enjoy seeing me tortured."

"Have they adopted you?"

"I don't know what you mean."

"I have been adopted into this wigwam. That was what the belt of beads meant. Now my master, Sabbatis, is my 'little brother,' and I have to call the old woman my *nigawes*. That means mother — God forgive me! I suppose we should be thankful. James said that once we are adopted they will not harm us. I wish I knew where they have taken the others."

"I don't see how you stand it!" Miriam burst out. "I wouldn't call that old hag mother, no matter what they did to me!"

"Then you'd be very foolish," replied Susanna crisply. "There could be worse things. Anyway, 'tis not for long, just till James can arrange for the ransom money. A white woman just came by here, though, who says she's been in this place for ten months. She says they won't object if we wash our clothes down by the river. I'll see if I can find the children and we can make ourselves more fitten."

As the days went by Miriam decided that she could not have been adopted. She was fed and allowed to sleep and otherwise completely ignored. Susanna and James had been put straightway to work. Susanna, with her slight strength, sat all day braiding tumpline or stitching deerskin shirts for her "little brother." James labored somewhere at the edge of camp, while Peter Labaree had been taken away, presumably to Montreal. When Miriam, restless with inactivity, ventured to help Susanna, Sabbatis took the work out of her hand and sent her away. Did he mistrust her ability to do even such a simple task?

Back in her own wigwam, Miriam sat watching the women. There was no man in this family. Chogan

was apparently a widow, and her daughter still un-
wed. At least here was no master to drive her on, and
no Mehkoa to torment her. She had caught only a few
glimpses of the Indian boy. She had learned, without
surprise, that he was a person of importance, son of
one of the sagamores who surrounded the Grand
Sachem. Praise be, she need no longer concern herself
with him, but sometimes the constant vexation of the
trail seemed preferable to this boredom, this endless
waiting that was worse than the stifling existence inside the fort at Number Four.

She sat watching the women's expert fingers, and
in spite of herself, her interest was caught by the
bright beaded design that formed under Chogan's
needle. Her own fingers itched to try it.

"I could do that," she offered finally. Chogan stared
at her doubtfully. Miriam picked up a needle that
had fallen to the dirt floor, and wove it through the
air in a convincing gesture. Grudgingly the squaw
handed her an unfinished moccasin and indicated
where it should be stitched, then watched sharply and
with surprise as this "no-good white squaw" drew the
needle capably through the soft leather. After that
Miriam was allowed to work at the family trade of
moccasin making, though if an outsider appeared at
the door the work was snatched from her hands. The
occupation was better than idleness, and within a few

days she had progressed to applying the beads, painstakingly copying the Indian woman's designs. Even the old grandmother nodded and smacked her lips in approval. Only the Indian girl seemed to understand that it was boredom and not good will that had prompted Miriam's interest. Every day she managed, by her lithe strength and the arrogant perfection of every graceful gesture, to make Miriam feel clumsy and weak. Between the two girls the wary hostility never relaxed.

Gradually her own young strength reasserted itself. A summerlike mood lay over the village. The still pools by the river's edge reflected the first red leaves of the maples. The warm blue sky cooled at night into a soft blackness thick-clustered with stars. There was plenty of food; the Indians feasted and shared their bounty lavishly. The work was not too burdensome to women accustomed to settlement living. Little Polly and Sue, though they were led away every evening to sleep in a distant wigwam, were allowed to join their mother every morning. Polly clung close to her mother's skirt, and was content to sit motionless for hours holding the baby carefully in her arms while Susanna worked. Sue gradually found courage to join in the noisy games with the white and Indian ragamuffins that swarmed the village. Both little girls had color in their cheeks now, and their bare arms and legs looked rounder. The baby Captive, fed on walnut meats stewed in cornmeal, was beginning to coo and gurgle like a proper child. Their work done, Miriam and Susanna sometimes joined the wistful straggle of white women who scrubbed their rags of clothes at the river and stubbornly cherished a remnant of English decency amid the squalor of the camp.

Early one morning, Miriam and Susanna sat for a few moments outside the wigwam of Sabbatis. Susanna's eyes lifted from her work and searched the roadway beyond the huts, straining in the hope of seeing James, who occasionally was able to walk past the wigwam on his way to work and to stop for a hurried word.

"Have you seen your brother?" she demanded once of Sue, who had lured Polly into a game of hopscotch in the dusty roadway.

"I saw Vanus this morning, running races in the clearing," Sue called over her shoulder. "He had some dark stuff rubbed into his hair."

"Always with the Indians," Susanna sighed. "I don't like it. I must get to talk with James somehow."

"I don't see why you worry about Vanus," Miriam said carelessly. "He's better off than any of us. The Indians just spoil him."

Susanna shot her a bleak glance. " 'Tis that that worries me. If we don't get him away from here soon he'll be completely out of hand. And 'tis time he started school."

"What makes you so sure we're going to get away?" Miriam had to ask. "What's to prevent their keeping us here forever, like the rest of the captives?"

Susanna's lips tightened. "Because we are not going to be like the others. Most of them have stopped hoping or even caring. We will never stop trying, not for one moment, and sooner or later, James will find a way."

Looking at her sister, Miriam marveled again how that slight body could contain such resolution. No, Susanna would never be like the others. But what of herself? she wondered uneasily. Was her own courage proof against many weeks of empty waiting?

She looked up, startled to see that a strange figure had paused before the wigwam. He was a white man, with a face like yellow wax under a wide black hat. A robe of some heavy black stuff closed tight about his throat and dragged in the dust at his feet. His eyes, looking out from deep hollows in his gaunt face, regarded her sister and the baby with such a gentleness and a deep sadness as she had never seen in all her life.

"The infant goes well?" he inquired haltingly.

"She is doing well, thank you," Susanna replied with a wariness in her tone that was unlike her usual frank

64

response. The tall man stood silent for a moment, and then, sensing her rebuff, turned away. As little Sue hopped carelessly into his path, he laid one hand briefly on her curly head.

"Who is he?" whispered Miriam, as he continued on his way.

"He is a priest," answered Susanna shortly.

"You mean — a Catholic?" Miriam recoiled from the word with all the prejudice of her Puritan upbringing.

"What did you expect? Didn't you know that the French are all Papists?"

"I never thought about it. But this man — his face is so kind —"

"They burned Hugh Latimer at the stake in England. Does that sound kind?"

Miriam was silent, puzzled. Incongruously, through this alien village, came the sound of a churchbell. Past the wigwam where they sat drifted little clusters of Indian women and children and an occasional aged brave, all following the summons of the tolling bell.

"I declare, it must be the Sabbath," said Susanna.

A scattering of white prisoners came by, bowing to the two English women like pathetic ghosts of decent churchgoers. A middle-aged couple, whom they already knew to be a Mr. and Mrs. Putnam from Northampton, paused for a moment.

65

"We're going to attend the mass, ma'am," Mr. Putnam offered. "If you've a mind to join us, we'd be happy to have you."

Susanna's shoulders stiffened. "I was not brought up to attend mass," she answered, and at her tone a trace of embarrassment crossed Mr. Putnam's face.

"No more were we," he answered stoutly. "But in this heathen place you got to cling to something."

Mrs. Putnam raised her eyes to meet Susanna's. "Right after they brought us in here," she explained, "our baby died. Father François, that's the priest, came and sat with us all night. And in the morning he gave her a Christian burial."

Tears of pity rose in Susanna's eyes, but she did not yield her disapproval. In the awkward silence Miriam ventured a question.

"This priest — how do the Indians allow a white prisoner so much influence?"

"Father François is no prisoner. He's a Jesuit priest. Saint Francis here is his parish."

"You mean he stays in this place of his own free will?"

"That's right. He says there's lots of Jesuits up north here, living in worse places than this. Some of them were very wealthy men back in France. They had a heap of schooling in fine universities and such, and then they sailed all the way over here to Canada just to save these worthless critters' souls. It's a marvel. Father François was even tortured by the Hurons once. You notice how he keeps one hand down at his side. All the same, he wouldn't leave."

The bell in the church steeple had stopped ringing, and Mrs. Putnam pulled her husband's sleeve.

"We got to hurry," she reminded him. "You sure you won't change your mind, Miz Johnson? There's a lot of comfort in the mass."

"Thank you," said Susanna. "We will hold our own service right here, the same as we always did at the fort. Try and find Vanus if you can, Miriam. We can't let him forget his catechism."

CHAPTER 6

They had lived in St. Francis for
three weeks when, early one evening, all the prisoners
were commanded to attend a Grand Council. Every
brave, old and young, in the village was present, with
the squaws ranged behind them along the walls. The
pipe was passed from mouth to mouth, filling the
lodge with its acrid, throat-catching smoke. The
Grand Sachem, impressive in his feathered bonnet,
spoke at great length to an audience so intently silent
that Miriam dared not even shift weight from one
cramped foot to the other. She had picked up a good
many Abenaki words by now, and the Indian gestures
were no longer meaningless. It was fairly easy to
figure out that the circle of braves who sat nearest the
fire were about to depart. Not on a raid this time, she
decided, because they were not painted, and there
was none of the mounting frenzy that would precede
a battle. It was a hunting trip, she interpreted, to some
place where many animals were dwelling. Mehkoa
was among the hunters. Time after time her eyes were

drawn back to that arrogant head with its boldly shaped features.

Suddenly, to her amazement, Mehkoa himself rose from the circle and turned to meet her gaze. With a start of panic she realized that he was coming toward her. Just in front of her, as she stepped involuntarily closer to Susanna, he stopped, standing very erect, and held out to her some object.

"Take it," prompted James, under his breath, and Miriam reached out her hand. It was a necklace of rare and valuable purple wampum, carved from the inside of the conch shell, each bead delicately fashioned by hand.

She heard Susanna draw in a sharp breath.

"What is it?" Miriam asked. "What does he want? Am I being adopted?"

Mehkoa spoke. "We go on big hunt. We away, squaws make ready log house — big — all new, like white man. When hunt over, white girl come live there. Squaw of Mehkoa."

Squaw! His meaning made its way, not into her mind, but into her veins like icy needles.

"Me — you mean — me *marry* you!" She thought she had screamed, but the words came out the barest breath.

Mehkoa heard them, however, and saw the unmistakable horror that drained her face white. In the depths of the dark eyes of the boy there was the merest flicker. Not a line of the young face changed, but that carved mask seemed to darken as though a shadow fell upon it. For one dreadful moment Miriam stared. Then, in blind terror and fury, she flung the necklace to the ground and turned and ran, past the motionless figures, down the dark alley, into her own wigwam. The ancient squaw, roused from her nap, looked on with unblinking eyes as Miriam flung herself sobbing on the pile of blankets.

There Susanna and James found her when they themselves were at last free to leave the Council. Susanna bent and gathered Miriam into her arms as though she were little Sue. James stood inside the wigwam door with both concern and disapproval on his face.

"You are not to scold the child," protested Susanna. " 'Twas a terrible shock, coming so unexpected-like."

"I understand that, my dear," James answered her. "I still say 'twas a pity she had to show it so plainly. When we are dealing with enemies it is well sometimes to respect their ways."

Miriam stiffened. "You mean you would have stood by and let them marry me off to that horrible savage?"

"Certainly not. There was no talk of marrying tonight. If you could have concealed your dread, we would have had time in our favor. As it is, our time is short, and truthfully, I am not sure what we can do."

"I don't understand," Miriam faltered. "How can anything I have done make things worse than they have been all this time? *Nothing* could be worse than having to marry an Indian!"

"Mehkoa thought he was doing you a great honor," Susanna explained. "They all thought so. That is why you were never adopted or given any real work to do, because Mehkoa had spoken for you and he is their favorite. But now you have shamed him before the whole tribe, and the women say you will never be forgiven for it."

"What is more," added James, "when you ran out of the lodge, Mehkoa announced that he no longer

71

wanted you on any terms, and he stalked out himself. The Indians consider that very childish behavior. Mehkoa is in disgrace with his father and with his own people. 'Tis that I am afraid of."

"We shouldn't hatchel the child like this," said Susanna. "She only did what any Godfearing woman would."

The two Indian women, coming into the wigwam, glared balefully at the intruders. With a last tightening of her arms, Susanna released her sister and left her. Shrinking, Miriam met the gaze of her Indian family. The girl's eyes glittered triumphantly, not so much with hatred as with contempt. Chogan's face was ugly.

She pointed to the dying fire, and with a threatening gesture ordered Miriam to stir the embers. When Miriam, in confusion, moved too slowly, she emphasized the order with a vicious kick at the girl's shin. The stab of pain taught Miriam more clearly than James's warning that from now on her life in the village was to be a far different affair.

Worse calamity befell them next morning. At dawn the Indian women went out to watch the departure of the hunting party, and taking advantage of their absence, Miriam crept to the wigwam of Sabbatis in search of her sister. She had just reached the wigwam when two braves came to greet Susanna, escorting between them little Sylvanus, clad in new deerskin jacket and leggings.

"Look, Ma," he boasted. "I got a new bow and five arrows all my own. I'm going to kill a deer. Maybe even a bear."

"Maybe you will," rallied Susanna, her voice trembling with foreboding, "when you're big enough."

"I'm big enough now. I'm going to be a sannup pretty soon. You just wait and see if I don't bring back a deer."

"What are you talking about, Vanus?" demanded Susanna, her eyes darting to the Indians in suspicion.

"I'm not Vanus any more. I'm Matguas now. That means Rabbit."

"He big man now," grinned an Indian. "He go big hunt."

"Big man!" cried Susanna. "He's only a little boy — only six years old! He can't go on a hunt with men!"

"Six year plenty big," nodded the Indian. "Indian boy go five year, sometime."

"Matguas smart boy. Make good sannup," agreed the other.

"Indeed he won't!" cried Susanna, forgetting all caution. "You can't take a child like this. I shan't allow it."

The grins vanished from the Indians' faces. Sylvanus, his fine prospects threatened, broke into shrill protest.

"You can't stop me! I'm not Vanus any more. I'm Matguas. I'm an Indian now!"

"Stop talking nonsense, Vanus. Where is your father? Where is Captain Johnson?"

One Indian shrugged. "White Captain make trouble," the other admitted. "Him tied in big wigwam. Not go out now."

Susanna's hands went to her throat. She tried another tactic.

"A child will just be in your way," she coaxed. "His legs will give out. He talks big, but he's only — "

"Go now," broke in the Indian roughly. "No talk more."

"Vanus!" sobbed his mother, throwing her arms around the child. Sylvanus lifted his brown cheeks for her kiss as unconcernedly as though he were leaving for an hour's play. Then he broke from her and trotted away with the Indians. But as Susanna ran after him along the pathway, he turned back, and for the first time his blue eyes were clouded with doubt.

" 'Tis all right, isn't it, Ma?" he quavered. "What are you crying about?"

The crack in his childish bravado steadied Susanna. Catching Miriam's arm in a grip that made the girl gasp, Susanna fought for a voice that would reassure him.

" 'Tis all right, Vanus," she managed finally. "Be a good boy, and be sure to say your prayers every night."

Miriam's own troubles were blotted out in her sister's anguish. But she was not allowed any time to attempt to comfort Susanna. Chogan, returning, set her to work with lashing tongue and a cuff that left her ear throbbing. From that morning on there were no more bright beaded designs or soft skins to work on. Instead she lugged heavy buckets of water, scoured greasy cooking pots with dirt and pebbles, and learned with an aching head and scarred shins that the wood for the fire had better not run short.

One morning, under a vicious yank, the too often scrubbed calico dress ripped irretrievably, and Miriam was forced to put on the castoff leather shirt and skirt that were flung at her. These foul-smelling Indian garments, far more than the back-breaking work, undermined her courage. They symbolized for her all the shame of captivity. In her own dress she had retained her white pride, but how could she even feel like a Willard inside these heathen clothes? Tears of weariness and self-pity dropped on the matted fringe.

I am no better that the others, she thought. In a little while anyone would have to look close to tell me from a squaw, and I won't even care.

That night a shriveled old sannup with a game leg that kept him from the hunt visited the wigwam. He watched as Miriam hoisted a heavy kettle, and he prodded with a hard finger to test the muscle in her arm. When he had gone Chogan thrust a leering face close to Miriam's.

"You like?" she croaked. "Him better young sagamore?" And at Miriam's question she burst into a malicious cackle.

Pretending to be in need of firewood, Miriam fled to Susanna's wigwam. As she neared it, she heard low voices in the darkness, and stopped short, unable to believe her ears. Susanna and her husband James stood in the shadow beside the wigwam, and they were quarreling in tense whispers. Never in her entire life had Miriam heard a bitter word between these two. For all her determination, Susanna had never dreamed of setting her will against James, and he, on his part, would have given her anything she asked without stopping to count the cost. Yet here in the darkness, in a voice choked with weeping, Susanna was insisting, and James was refusing in anger. Miriam, both puzzled and frightened, crept away, ashamed of having eavesdropped.

Next morning she discovered the cause of their argument. It was barely daybreak when a rough hand

and a prodding toe jerked her from sleep. Chogan stood over her. Miriam stumbled to her feet and followed the squaw out the door, between the shadowy wigwams, down the path to the river. There James and Susanna waited, standing close together in the bitter frost, James's arm about his wife's shoulder. Miriam's first thought was one of relief. These two were no longer in disagreement. Then the strain on both their faces blotted out her relief. She saw the canoe bobbing softly against the pebbles, held by two Indians who waited, paddles in hand. In the bottom of the canoe, huddled under blankets, Polly and Sue crouched, with terrified faces.

Susanna broke gently from James's embrace and came to lay both hands on her sister's arms. "You are not to be worried, Miriam," she said earnestly. "James has managed to persuade them to take you to Montreal. They would not listen to him before, when Mehkoa had spoken for you. Now they have no use for you and think they might as well sell you to the French. And once he is there, James can begin to arrange with Massachusetts for our ransom."

Miriam hugged her sister in joy. "Worried!" she cried. "To get away from this dreadful place? 'Tis what we have hoped for all along."

Susanna said nothing, and over her shoulder Miriam saw James's face, haggard as an old man's.

"What is it?" she asked, drawing back. Susanna appealed hesitantly to James, who refused to help her.

" 'Tis nothing," explained Susanna finally. "Just that Sabbatis will not let me go at present. Only you and James, and the little girls."

"And leave you alone — in this place? Have you lost your mind, Susanna? How could you consider such a thing, James?"

James clenched his hands. "I have said all I can," he groaned. "They are taking the children away, no matter what I do."

"James knows it is best this way," Susanna went on. "It is his only chance to get through to the colonies. You must see, both of you, that there may not be another chance. I am perfectly safe here. Sabbatis treats me fairly, and I could not leave anyway till Sylvanus comes back from the hunt. When the French have made a good offer, they will let me come fast enough."

Afterwards Miriam was glad to remember that she had spoken without thinking. "Then let James go. And the girls. I'm not going without you."

"Oh, I can't go on fighting both of you," cried poor Susanna. "Don't you see, Miriam, 'twas a miracle he could persuade them. You have to go. They are planning to marry you off. Nobody wants you now, but that old man who needs a squaw to do his work. Even one more day and you might never get away at all. We can't afford to waste time like this."

Chogan, sensing that the promised money might be slipping from her grasp, took a menacing step toward the sisters. "No talk. No-good squaw go now," she ordered. One of the Indians lifted his paddle and grunted impatiently. The sound roused James from his indecision.

"Get in the canoe, Miriam," he ordered harshly.

Miriam clung to her sister, weeping, until Susanna, with dry eyes, pushed her away. Then the girl ran blindly to the canoe, climbed in beside the bewildered children, and hid her face against Polly. In a moment she felt the canoe rock beneath James's step, and then move in one sweeping shove away from the shore. At the same instant, wails of realization burst from Polly and Sue. Miriam and James bent automatically to muffle their cries. The canoe shot toward a bend in the river, and looking back, they watched the frail figure standing gallantly on the shore, till Susanna was lost to their sight.

CHAPTER 7

"THERE IS Montreal," said James. "We shall reach it before nightfall."

Miriam shook off the sleep that dragged at her and struggled to sit up. The Indians made no protest; here on the broad St. Lawrence River they had no need for caution. She gazed at the unknown French city whose name, ever since childhood, had meant to her only hatred and terror. To a girl who had spent her entire life in the sparsely settled New Hampshire valley, it appeared huge and threatening. Behind the great stone walls rose black gabled roofs, pointed church steeples, two massive stone towers, and looming over them all, a menacing rocky hill.

"It looks frightening." She shuddered. "Is it made all of stone?"

"It will take a strong force to capture it," commented James, studying the distant walls with a soldier's eye.

"Why must we try to capture this place, so far from home?" Miriam asked, voicing a question that had

80

long puzzled her. "Why shouldn't there be room on this huge continent for both the French and the English to live peaceably?"

James scowled. "King Louis of France is determined to be master of this entire continent," he said sternly. "All this country belongs by first claim to King George, yet the French are rapidly surrounding us to the west and even to the south. What right have they to hem us in to the few miles between here and the coast? They would soon push us into the ocean. Already they have taken control of the great waterways to the west and the rich fur trade. Would you have us sit idle while they send the Indians to sack and burn our houses, and even offer money for our scalps?"

It had been disloyal even to question, Miriam realized, gazing fearfully back at the dark stone towers. As the canoe drew nearer she could see stretched on either side along the banks of the river rows of little houses, low and peak-roofed, gleaming white in the afternoon sun. These tidy peaceful houses were somehow reassuring.

Little Polly and Sue lay crumpled in the bottom of the canoe, not knowing or caring that the end of the journey was in sight. After that last glimpse of their mother on the bank of the river at St. Francis they had cried themselves into an exhausted slumber. James, wrapped in bitter silence, had seemed not even

81

to notice their sobs, or the tears that Miriam could not hold back. Leaving Susanna had robbed them all of their courage. More than ever they realized how her spirit had upheld them through all the days of their captivity.

It was almost dark and bitterly cold when the canoe scraped the landing beach at Montreal. The little girls were shaken out of their slumber and half dragged out of the canoe to stand huddled close together, shivering in the sharp gusts of wind that whistled through their deerskin jackets. One Indian vanished in the dusk and presently returned with three soldiers, who marshaled the group of prisoners along the beach, through a heavy gate, into a dimly lighted shed. There they waited. Outside they heard a medley of French and Indian as their captors carried on a stubborn transaction. Then there was silence for a long time, until the stamp of heavy boots on the stone pavement told them that the soldiers were returning. Apparently the Indians had concluded their bargain, for they were nowhere to be seen. There was a new French soldier, in impressive white uniform, who must be of higher rank.

Accustomed to their aloof and uncommunicative Indian captors, Miriam found these French white men terrifying, with their dark beards, their loud voices, their intrusive black eyes. One young soldier stared boldly at her in a way that was even more disturbing than Mehkoa's inscrutable glance. This boy took in every detail of her bedraggled clothing, and then tossed over his shoulder some remark that provoked a loud burst of laughter. The officer scowled at him and then spoke courteously to James.

Miriam and James exchanged a look of dismay as they understood the officer's meaning. They were all to be separated; each one of them had been privately purchased. After a quick fire of directions, one of the soldiers hoisted a terrified Polly to his shoulder, and another abruptly held out his hand to Sue. Sue hid both hands behind her, and shrank against her father, the ready tears welling up in her eyes. James laid a hand on his daughter's head.

"Where is she going?" he asked, loudly and distinctly.

"A *les bonnes Soeurs de la Congrégation de Notre-Dame,*" the officer replied, with considerate slowness.

"*Les bonnes soeurs,*" repeated James, knitting his forehead. "I think they are taking you to a convent, Susanna. In that case you need not be afraid at all. Those good women will be kind to you. Go with him, my dear, and be a good, obedient girl. Trust in God, all of you, and I am sure that we shall all be together in a short time."

"But when?" Miriam demanded in panic. "How

83

will you know where to find us in this great city, James?"

"I shall find you, never fear," James promised. "We can do nothing tonight. Tomorrow I shall find someone who speaks English. I am sure that these are reasonable people and that there will be no trouble at all. Have faith, Miriam."

Gathering what courage she could from James's assurance, Miriam followed the beckoning soldier out the door into the dark roadway. Sue and Polly were already out of sight. Stumbling to keep up with him on the uneven pavestones, she could see nothing on either side but close dark walls that seemed to tower to the sky. They turned into a wider street that climbed with a sharp rise. She was out of breath when the soldier stopped and rapped with the butt of his musket on a shadowy doorway. As the door swung open, he pushed Miriam ahead of him over the threshold.

Miriam stood blinking at a scene so beautiful that it had to be a dream. There was warmth and light, and the long-remembered fragrance of new bread. There was a roaring fire in a wide stone hearth hung about with copper and pewter. There were scrubbed floors and a red and blue braided rug. Could this be an enemy country, where every object was so dear and familiar?

But the voices were not at all familiar. With a rapid, high-pitched jabbering that made her ears ring, a half-dozen women crowded around her, all talking at once and flashing their dark eyes and white teeth. The soldier, with a grin and a wave of his hand, closed the door and left her alone with them.

She stood with her back against the door and let them stare. They were as inquisitive as the Indian women, but they showed no signs of wanting to tear her to pieces, or even to step closer. Their laughter died away. One young woman stepped back, holding her pretty uptilted nose with dainty fingers, and the others tittered. Miserably, Miriam saw herself through their eyes. The leather skirt was caked with mud from the last portage. Her hair was matted and uncombed, her face streaked with tears, her bare feet calloused and dirty. And the stench of the deerskin jacket in this hot room was shameful.

There's more than one way of running a gantlet, she thought. At least the Indians give you a chance to run.

How long she could stand there meekly enduring their inspection, she was beginning to wonder, when a door opened and a step caused the women to jump back with instant respect. Into the cricle advanced a woman, such a figure as Miriam had never encountered in all her life.

She had a beautiful shell-white face and a tall haughty carriage. Her clothes were incredible, swaying billows of gleaming green with frothy white ruffles and a flash of gold and jewels at throat and wrist. Her hair was utterly astonishing, snow-white, topped by a brilliant bird's feather. Most unbelievable of all, she spoke in English stressing the syllables oddly.

"Your name, girl?" Her voice was sharp.

"Miriam Willard, ma'am," the girl answered, and then, as the woman looked puzzled, "Captain James Johnson is my brother-in-law, and he will come for me tomorrow."

The woman lifted one eyebrow. Her chill blue eyes flicked over Miriam from matted hair to grimy toe. *"Incroyable!"* she murmured. "You must take those clothes off at once. And I suppose you are hungry?"

"Not especially," Miriam lied, her pride stiffening.

The woman shrugged. "Why you English prisoners are any concern of ours I fail to understand. But Monsieur Du Quesne, my husband, has most generously agreed to allow you to stay here till your ransom can be arranged."

"That is very kind of him, ma'am," responded Miriam, seeing that gratitude was expected, however little she might feel. "I am sure I shall not have to trouble you for long."

"That we shall see. In the meantime, I expect you to make yourself useful."

"Indeed I shall try, ma'am."

The woman turned to the others, who, Miriam now realized, must be servants, and issued a series of orders in rapid French. When their mistress's voluminous skirts had swished through the doorway, the women fell to work. Into the center of the kitchen they dragged a large wooden tub and filled it with steaming water from the kettle. Then they stepped back, pointing from Miriam to the tub, as though she were a dim-witted creature who might not understand what it was all about.

They can think I'm stupid if they like, thought Miriam stubbornly. If they expect me to undress while they all stand and watch me and laugh at me, they can wait all night. Even the Indians had more shame.

All at once, a young girl stepped out from the circle. "*Sortez-vous!*" she ordered, shooing the others away like chickens. Seizing a red blanket from a chest near the hearth, she held it wide between her outstretched arms, making a screen between Miriam and the rest of the room. "*Allons!*" she smiled.

The other women laughed good-naturedly and moved away. Miriam's defiance suddenly melted in surprise and gratitude. The face that twinkled back at her over the red blanket was frank and friendly, without a hint of malice. The girl had round rosy cheeks and wiry black hair that crinkled crisply all over her head. The small pointed teeth that stuck crookedly out in front and her eyes, shiny as black buttons, made Miriam think of a little chipmunk, and all the girl's motions seemed to be as merry and quick. A lump rose treacherously in Miriam's throat, and she began hurriedly to untie the deerhide thongs.

Slipping off her clothes as fast as possible, she leaped for the tub, and gasped as she crouched down into the scalding water.

Even the sidelong glances of amusement that still needled her could not entirely spoil the bliss of hot water and good yellow soap. Miriam rubbed the heavy suds into her matted hair, relishing the sharp sting on her eyelids and the bitter taste in her mouth. She scrubbed until her skin smarted and her pores had given up the last trace of Indian. The thick towel that the French girl warmed at the hearth wrapped all the way round her. Then there were clean, fresh-smelling clothes, a sturdy petticoat, a short blue home-spun skirt, and a white cloth bodice, thick white stockings, and real leather boots. The girl brought her a comb for her hair, and a soft ribbon to tie it back. When it was all done, she stood back and stared at Miriam with flattering delight.

"*Mais — vous êtes belle!*" she cried, so generously that Miriam's heart went out to her. She was far from whatever *belle* meant, she knew, even in these good clothes. There was no hiding her bony arms and her brown roughened skin. But the word did her good, nonetheless.

"Thank you," she said shyly, the first word she had dared to speak.

"Meeriam?" the girl questioned, giving the word an

odd twist. *"Je m'appelle Hortense."*

"Hortense," Miriam attempted. "Thank you, Hortense."

At one corner of the long wooden table they set for her a plate piled high with roasted potatoes and cabbage and some white baked fish. There were thick slices of crusty bread and a pewter mug of yellow milk. No wonder all these women looked so plump and pink-cheeked! Miriam dared not eat half of it. She had learned painfully in the wilderness how unwise it could be to feast on an empty stomach.

As she ate, the kitchen became a bustle of activity. Evidently the evening meal was about to be served in some other room of the house, and the women had no more time to waste on the newcomer. Left alone at the corner of the table, Miriam watched their quick darting figures, so different from the deliberate motions of the Indian squaws or the sober efficiency of the women at Charlestown. These women seemed to have energy to spare. They got in each other's way, and laughed and twitched their skirts and rolled their eyes and kept up a constant chatter. The noise and the high laughter made Miriam feel giddy. The kitchen wavered before her eyes, and she gripped the table edge hard with both hands. Suddenly Hortense noticed.

"Tch, tch!" she clucked, and slipping a hand under

Miriam's elbow, she drew her up from the bench and led her to a sort of ladder in the corner of the room, seizing a candle from the shelf as she passed.

The loft to which they climbed was far more spacious and well furnished than the one in which Miriam had slept at Number Four. There was a row of plump mattresses on the floor, and to one of these Hortense led her.

"*C'est à moi,*" she explained, and then, on impulse, she bent forward and touched the mattress. "*Le lit,*" she said carefully. "*C'est le lit.*"

"Lee," repeated Miriam. Then she too bent forward and touched the mat. "In English, it is bed," she told Hortense. "A bed."

"Baid," repeated Hortense. Her round face wrinkled up with pleasure. Miriam took the stuff of the blue homespun skirt in her hands. "Dress," she said. "Dress."

"*C'est la robe,*" the French girl answered. "*La robe* — dr–r–ess.*"

They grinned at each other with mutual pride. "I'm too sleepy to learn any more tonight. But thank you — oh Hortense, thank you so much!" Hortense nodded. There was no doubt about the meaning of that heart-felt word. Then she put the candle on the floor near the mat and popped down the loft entrance, leaving Miriam alone.

Relaxing in a real bed again, Miriam's conscience pricked her. Was there something shameless about her? Here she had been sold into slavery. Was it proper to relish enemy food and snuggle into a soft bed like an animal that cared for nothing but its own comfort? What would Susanna have done? The memory of Susanna sent a real shaft of pain through her content.

Susanna would like Hortense, she assured herself. Hortense cannot possibly be an enemy.

Her mind was hazy with sleep. She could not concentrate on Susanna far away in the wilderness. In spite of herself her natural optimism had bounced back. Now that it was over, her elastic young spirit shed that time of fear and degradation as easily as she had cast aside the deerskin jacket. There was nothing to fear in this place, and for the first time since the night of the party at Number Four her last thought of the morrow was not of foreboding but of anticipation.

CHAPTER 8

WHEN MIRIAM woke it was still dark, and the loft was barely visible in the smoky candlelight. The chattering had begun again, but in whispers and subdued giggles. The women were rousing from the row of mattresses and getting dressed. Hortense, sitting on the edge of the mat she had shared with Miriam, was lost in the folds of the petticoat she was pulling over her head. The bobbing black curls and plump round cheeks emerged in a moment, and her black eyes twinkled at Miriam. Miriam dragged herself up, though she could have slept straight through the day, and pulled on her own dress and the leather shoes that were far too big. She followed the others down the loft ladder, took her turn at washing her face in the big basin, and sat down at the table. After a few moments' bustle, breakfast was ready, porridge and thick yellow cream, and a mug of indescribably luscious brew called chocolate, dark and rich and sweet.

This morning the other women had lost their curiosity and quite casually accepted her as one of them. She was tossed a towel and she set to wiping plates and spoons, and then to shining a set of pewter mugs, and for some time she worked in a corner undisturbed. Then Hortense beckoned to her.

The French girl was deftly arranging on a brass tray a delicate white china cup and plate, thin silver spoons, a little pot of chocolate and two crusty rolls. A late breakfast for the lady of the house, Miriam guessed. She followed Hortense with some curiosity. She had discarded her timidity with the disgraceful Indian clothes. Those icy blue eyes would not fluster her so easily this morning. The two girls passed from the kitchen into a sitting room that made Miriam gasp. Such elegance! She glimpsed a fine stuffed sofa, chairs of dark polished wood, hangings of deep red velvet. Beyond this room they mounted a short flight of stairs into a narrow hallway, and Hortense opened a door into a small chamber.

That anyone in the world had such a room merely for sleeping was beyond imagination. It was all white and pale blue. There were thick creamy rugs on a blue-painted floor. The windows and a little dressing table were hung with white draperies ending in a long netted fringe. There was a wide four-poster bed with full white draw curtains and deep scalloped valances. In the center of the bed, under a fringed and embroidered coverlet and propped up against a

94

mass of ruffled pillows, sat not the formidable woman
Miriam expected but the prettiest girl she had ever
seen. She was pink and white and fragile as a china
figurine, her eyes like blue flowers, and her hair a fine
powdery gold mist against the pillows. The blue eyes
darted past Hortense and the tray, and went wide
at the sight of Miriam. For a long moment the two
girls stared at each other, each too dumfounded to
speak. Then the girl on the bed broke into a flood of
French, as rapid as the chatter in the kitchen, but
softer, with a hint of a lisp that reminded Miriam of
Polly. Hortense laughed, plumped the tray down
on the bed, and gave an explanation. The girl turned
to Miriam.

"You no speak *français?*" she demanded. Miriam

shook her head. The girl laughed, showing a row of perfect small teeth. "It no matter. I speak the English with you. You surprise — *n'est-ce pas?*"

For the first time since she had left James at the landing place Miriam could speak her own tongue freely, and the words rushed out with all the old frankness.

"Everything in Montreal surprises me. It is all so different from what I expected." Especially you, she almost added, but remembered her manners in time.

The girl was delighted. "You like it — no?"

"I haven't seen anything but this house. 'Tis the most beautiful house I have ever seen."

"It is one of best houses in Montreal. We get everything from France — chairs, tables, dishes, everything. Where you come from, you not have house like this?"

"Goodness no! At Number Four the men themselves had to build the houses out of logs."

"Number Four? What is that?" The white forehead wrinkled.

"That is the name they gave our settlement at first. Now it is called Charlestown."

The girl motioned to a footstool near the bed. "You stay here with me while I eat. Tell me about this — this Number Four."

Hortense broke in with a protest, obviously explaining that Miriam was expected to work in the kitchen.

The laughter went out of the girl's face, the red lips pouted, and for an instant there was the faintest echo of Madame Du Quesne in her blue eyes and in the quick imperious gesture. Hortense did not argue; she curtsied and was out the door in a flash, leaving Miriam behind.

"Now," said the French girl, nestling back among the pillows, her sunny nature restored. "You tell to me. How you come to be with the Indians? Did they treat you bad?"

Where could she begin? Miriam wondered. What words could possibly give this exquisite creature an inkling of what it was like to march cold and hungry, covered with mud and insect bites, along a forest trail? Instead she decided to tell about the settlement at Charlestown. Even that sounded outlandish enough, here in this dainty room, but her story found an eager audience. Encouraged by those astonished blue eyes and the soft gasps of amazement, the words began to pour out. The joy of having someone her own age to talk to! She had forgotten the circumstances, the fact that she was a prisoner, and she was living again the night of the dance at Number Four, when the door opened, and the mistress of the house stepped into the room.

She surveyed the two girls with displeasure, and broke into a sharp hailstorm of words and gestures that indicated plainly that it was high time to be up and about. The girl on the bed was not in the least cowed by this tirade. She pouted prettily.

"Oh, Maman, she is so droll, this Meeriam."

It was Miriam's turn to feel that icy glance, and she stood uncomfortably waiting for the wrath to descend on her head.

"They have given you some work to do?" queried Madame.

"Yes, ma'am," Miriam answered meekly, trying to gauge whether she could slip between the wide-spread skirts and the doorway. But the girl on the bed had other plans.

"But, Maman, I wish her to stay here with me!"

The older woman considered this for a moment. Then she turned to Miriam. "Can you read and write the English?" she demanded.

"Why of course, ma'am."

"What can you read?" persisted Madame.

"I have read the Bible all the way through twice, and the sermons of Cotton Mather." That was everything she had found to devour in her father's cabin, but the list made slight impression on this woman.

"Perhaps it will do," she said finally. "I should like my daughter to learn to read the English and to speak it correctly. When I was her age there was an English sister at the school who taught us very carefully. She

98

was very particular about how we spoke. But she has died, and the sisters do not bother any longer. Felicité speaks a little, as you see, but she is lazy. I shall get a book of English from the sisters, and you shall teach her to read."

"Oh, I should like to try, ma'am," cried Miriam eagerly. "I always helped the little girls at home."

"Then perhaps we shall get some good out of you after all," concluded Madame. "You will come up here every morning and teach Felicité for two hours."

"Two hours!" squealed Felicité in consternation. "But, Maman — !" Her protest was broken off by a sharp rebuke, and Madame, the business settled, swept out of the room.

Felicité was sulky. "What good is it to read the English? Who I ever speak English to anyway? Everybody speaks *français*."

"You might like it," coaxed Miriam.

"Maman, she always say someday we go back to France — Paris — and then we visit London. But I know we stay right here. I marry Pierre, have French babies. What I need the English for?"

Madame's plans were law, however. From that morning Miriam became a teacher and Felicité a reluctant pupil. At first it seemed to Miriam pure enchantment to sit in that pretty room, to watch Felicité, with her appealing birdlike ways, to have a fine leather-bound book to read. But that it was not going to be an easy task to teach this pupil she soon began to suspect. Four-year-old Sue was quicker at her letters. Felicité's bright eyes and attention darted everywhere, but came to rest invariably on herself, on the shadow of a curl against the wall, on a fingernail threatened by a tiny snag, on the ruffles that had to fall just so over her dainty wrist. Over and over Miriam pulled her back to the words on the page — the same words every day, for they seemed to make no progress whatsoever. She must be a very poor teacher, Miriam decided. Surely anyone so delicate and beautiful as Felicité could not be — no, it was disloyal to even think the word. The failure must be her own.

Meanwhile, down below in the kitchen, another kind of education was in progress. The kitchen was still the place where Miriam properly belonged, and once the two hours with Felicité were over she returned there and took up her share of the work. Here she became both teacher and pupil, for Hortense was quick to follow up that first lesson in the loft. Now as they washed the dishes, and peeled potatoes, and polished the brass and copper, side by side, the tongues of the two girls wagged merrily. These lessons were pure fun. Where Felicité puckered her pretty forehead over one phrase, Hortense picked up dozens of words in a day, and generously tossed back to Miriam dozens of French words in return. She marveled at Hortense. This kitchen maid who admitted she could neither read nor write and had no reason in the world for wanting to speak a foreign tongue grasped the words and stored them away like the quick little squirrel she resembled, just for the fun of it. The hours passed quickly as they jabbered in a ridiculous mixture of languages, and often Hortense doubled up in merriment over Miriam's mistakes. But Miriam worked in earnest. Every day there was less English and more French in the mixture. Gradually both Hortense and Felicité lapsed into their native tongue, and Miriam rapidly learned to follow.

As one day after another went by, however, and the novelty of the household no longer distracted all her thoughts, a deep uneasiness began to increase in Miriam's mind. Still no word from James. Surely something had gone wrong with his plans. And where were the little girls? They might not have been so lucky as she. For she had been lucky beyond anything she could have dreamed. It was hard to remember that she was a prisoner, and that Montreal was a dreaded and evil city. Surely it was treacherous of her, but she had to admit that she found every feature of this new experience exciting. If only she could know about the others. Not knowing was the one shadow that dimmed this adventure.

"You are not happy," Hortense accused her, as they sat one afternoon filling the great preserving crocks with crisp green cucumber slices. "We are not being good to you?"

Miriam looked into the anxious black eyes of her new friend. "Oh, Hortense, you are being good to me! I like it here, truly I do. But I am worried about the others. I told you my sister had to stay behind with the Indians, but we thought it would not be for long. And if I could only know what they have done with the little girls!"

"But of course. I would feel the same. Madame does not tell you anything?"

"I hardly ever see Madame, and then she is always giving orders. I don't dare ask her. She is so — so — "

Hortense laughed. "I know. We find out for ourselves. I ask Jules when he comes tonight."

"Jules?"

Hortense's eyes danced. "Jules is my — " She hesitated, and a rosy blush supplied the word she could not find. "He is a habitant," she went on hurriedly. "He owns one hundred arpents of land, and he already has two horses and five cows. He is very smart man, my Jules."

Miriam stared at her in surprise. Felicité of course

had any number of admirers. They drove up to the great front door in carriages, and the servants peeked through the drawing-room curtains and commented on this one and that one. It was hard to make Felicité stop chattering about her drives and her parties long enough to concentrate on an English sentence. But it had never occurred to Miriam that Hortense might have a life of her own beyond this kitchen. She felt a quick prick of envy.

The envy stirred again when Jules arrived after supper. There was quite a flurry in the kitchen as he stepped in out of the chilly night. The women greeted him familiarly, and made way for Hortense with good-natured, outspoken jibes that made her cheeks flame. Miriam stared curiously. Yes, Jules was unmistakably a farmer, and quite as certainly successful and self-confident. His shoulders strained the rough homespun coat, his waist was stocky under the red woolen sash. Black hair curled tightly under the red cap, and his white teeth flashed in his broad swarthy face. He was totally unlike the young man she remembered so well; yet, watching Jules and Hortense standing together just inside the kitchen door, Miriam knew exactly how they felt. She herself stood all at once inside another door, and Phineas Whitney's face came before her memory so clearly that her heart gave a leap. Would she ever know again the magic that wove such a spell about a man and a girl that they could stand completely alone in a room full of people?

Hortense had not forgotten her completely, however. She came back to Miriam a little later with a small frown between her eyes.

"Jules does not know about your little girls," she said. "He will find out for us tomorrow, perhaps. But he has heard about your brother, the English captain."

"What about him?" Miriam begged.

"They have put him in the prison. But don't look like that, Miriam. Jules says they often keep English prisoners there. He will try to find out more. You must not worry about it."

Miriam shivered in the warm kitchen. She had felt all along that it was treacherous of her to enjoy this place. Now the fragrant steam rising from the hearth sickened her. It was all an illusion, this luxury she had begun to take for granted. If James were in prison, there was no hope that Susanna could escape from St. Francis. They were all separated and helpless, and what hope was there that they would ever go home again?

"Come, Miriam," coaxed Hortense. "It is not so bad. I think you like Montreal, when you know it better. Besides, tomorrow night Jules will come back, and maybe you be surprised. You see."

CHAPTER 9

"FINISHED already?" inquired Hortense, as Miriam came back to the kitchen next morning.

"Madame cut the lesson short," Miriam responded. "They are going out for a drive."

"You are still sad, *n'est-ce pas?*" observed Hortense. "That is not good on a morning like this."

On the tip of Miriam's tongue, ready to pour out to any sympathetic ear, was the latest snub that Madame Du Quesne had inflicted. That morning Felicité had had a sudden impulse.

"Maman," she had begged, "let Miriam go with us to drive in the carriage. Think, Maman, she has never even ridden in such a carriage as ours!"

Madame's icy glance had flicked both the eager young faces. "You forget yourself, Felicité" was all she had said, but Miriam accepted the rebuke meant for her.

No doubt she had forgotten herself. How could she think that Felicité could really be her friend, when she was a prisoner and a servant? But she was a

Willard too, and wasn't a Willard good enough to ride in a carriage with a Du Quesne? However, something warned her that she had best keep this disappointment to herself. It would never occur to Hortense to have her feelings hurt because she wasn't invited for a drive in the carriage. Better to allow Hortense to assume that it was worry and not snubbed pride that dampened her spirits.

"I am going to take you to market with me," Hortense announced now. "They cannot expect you to work all the time, and you can help carry the vegetables. I ask Madame."

She was back in a moment with permission. Presently both girls set out, red wool scarves tied about their heads, baskets swinging on their arms. Miriam's spirits bounced upward. Shafts of sunlight slanted through the narrow street. Above the steep gabled rooftops the sky shone a brilliant October blue.

"That is the Mayor's house," Hortense pointed out, as they descended the hill past fine stone mansions. "And there is the Séminaire de Saint Sulpice."

Miriam stared curiously through the iron gateway. Beyond the stone building she caught a glimpse of quiet gardens between neat paths, of lovely old trees whose yellow leaves drifted gently into a tranquil pond. Against the high protecting walls branches had been carefully trained to spread in graceful patterns.

A priest in his dark robe was pruning a small fruit tree. How strange that men should have leisure to cultivate plants and trees not for sustenance at all, but merely for beauty! There was much about this place that she would like to ask Hortense, but the practical French words she had learned would never convey the questions that crowded her mind.

They came out on the Rue de St. Paul. Between this long street and the river were crowded the busy shops of shoemakers, gunsmiths, hatmakers, bakers, furriers, with their wares displayed in windows and doorways. Beyond these rose the dingy warehouses that fronted the water's edge. What a bustling there was everywhere! Housewives stepped briskly toward the market place, nodding and chatting to one another. Servants in short skirts and bodices like her own and matrons in flounces, with elaborately curled and powdered hair, mingled with soldiers in white uniforms laced with black, and priests in their dark robes. Along the street came two smiling Sisters, in gray robes, marshaling a group of little girls in neat wool dresses. As they passed, Miriam stopped to stare at the children's smooth dark braids.

"Why, they are Indian children!" she exclaimed.

"But of course," answered Hortense. "They belong to the School."

A school for Indian children! Miriam had never

heard of such a thing. Back in Charlestown, in peace times, the Indian traders had sometimes been trailed by children, sly dirty little rascals, skittish as wild animals. "Keep an eye on them," the settlers' wives had said, "they can steal a loaf of bread quicker than you can wink." Who had ever seen Indian children like these happy little girls, scrubbed and decorous and smiling?

"What do they learn?" she asked wonderingly.

"The same as French girls, to sing hymns and paint pictures and sew and embroider. Indian girls have very clever fingers for sewing."

Miriam turned reluctantly from the charming procession to match the impatient stride of her friend. In a moment the Indians were forgotten as the sounds and colors and smells of the market place rose about her in such wealth. Housewives bargained shrilly over stalls piled high with golden carrots, glossy red apples, green lettuce and cabbage, and great orange pumpkins. Chickens squawked from wicker baskets. At the end of the row they stopped at the fish stall and Hortense selected a huge silver cod and four loathsome, snake-like eels. It was a pleasure to watch Hortense shop, to see her move from stall to stall, knowingly pinching the ripe fruit, keeping a sharp eye on the scales, battling good-naturedly for a bargain.

"They all know your name!" Miriam marveled. "Why, in my whole life I have never seen so many people as you have talked to just this morning."

Hortense did not hear her. She was standing stock still, her round cheeks quivering with excitement.

"*Regardez!*" she exclaimed. "The *coureur de bois!* I thought they had all gone!"

There was a burst of raucous, rollicking song. Down the street, four abreast, causing everyone to step aside to make room, strode four young men. One of the four, standing taller, singing louder, and striding a little more confidently than the others, captured every eye along the way. He was certainly the handsomest man Miriam had ever seen, yet he reminded her strikingly of Mehkoa. He moved with the same panther-like grace; his head and shoulders had the same arrogant lift. He was dressed almost like an Indian, too, in a deerskin jacket and leather breeches. He was burned dark as a redskin. But the black hair that curled tight and short against his head and the flashing white teeth proclaimed him a Frenchman, and no

109

ordinary habitant, by the way the humble folk moved out of his way.

As the girls watched, he checked his rapid stride and raised an arm in greeting. Following his smile, Miriam saw a sight calculated to cause any young man to stand still. Reined in on the opposite side of the street were two sleekly matched horses, and in a handsome carriage, behind a gold-braided footman, sat Madame Du Quesne, out for her morning drive. Beside her was her daughter Felicité, a pink and white vision of ruffles and bows and powdered curls. Her pretty lips parted in a bewitching smile as the *coureur* left his companions and bounded across the street. From the carriage a white-gloved hand stretched daintily, to which he bent with a flourish. Madame Du Quesne was almost unrecognizable, so transformed with nods and smiles. As the three chatted, Hortense and Miriam were not the only ones who gaped, forgetting business and manners.

"Ah — what a pair they make!" sighed Hortense. "Both so handsome, *n'est-ce pas?*"

"A pair?" echoed Miriam. "Felicité and that — that *coureur?*"

"If Madame has her way," laughed Hortense. "At least that's what they say. It won't be easy to snare that Pierre — he is a fox!"

"So that is the Pierre Felicité is always talking

110

about?" Miriam was shocked. "Why, he looks like a savage!"

"Oh, they all dress like that, the *coureur de bois*. It is part of the game. But that one — that Pierre — he is the grandson of Monsieur Laroche. His *grand-père* made a fortune in the fur trade. Any girl in New France would be proud to marry a Laroche."

"Even you, Hortense?" teased Miriam, amused at her friend's respectful tone.

Hortense was scandalized. "Pierre Laroche is a nobleman!" she said, flustered. "And even if he weren't, I'd never trade my Jules for any *coureur!*"

"What are *coureurs*, Hortense?"

"Fur traders. They go out on their own, not like the regular *voyageurs*. They think they are too good to work like ordinary folk. They leave their families and go off to trade with the Indians and get rich. A wild lot, most of them. They say they sleep in Indian wigwams, and eat dirty Indian food, and when they come back in the summer — pfft! — they spend everything they have earned."

The *coureur de bois*, Pierre, had rejoined his companions across the street, and Miriam lost sight of him in her absorption with the carriage and its occupants. She admired the way the sleek horses lifted their feet daintily from the road as though vain of the precious cargo they drew. Felicité was like a delicate flower.

111

What must it be like, to wear a dress like that, and to ride so elegantly, to have gloves on one's hands, and to know that all along the way people turned their heads and stared? Lost in envious wonder, Miriam had no idea that at the same time that she stared at Félicité, at least one pair of eyes was as keenly fixed on her own face. She was completely unaware of the soldier who had halted nearby. Had she stayed demurely at Hortense's side he would doubtless have gone on his way without daring to accost her. But as she stood, quite forgetful of herself, her attention was suddenly distracted by a familiar figure, a pair of erect shoulders and a head of grizzled hair. A little ahead of the carriage James Johnson, accompanied by a French soldier, was just turning away from the street into an alleyway. Without an instant's thought, Miriam flung herself into the roadway.

"James!" she screamed. "James! Wait!" That James was already out of sight and could not possibly hear her did not matter, nor that her English words and her headlong rush would startle the market place. The young soldier who had been eying her leaped into action. Before she had run three steps Miriam's flight was halted by a solid figure in her path.

Even in her excitement Miriam recognized the soldier who had stared at her so rudely that first night on the riverbank. But she could not bother with him now. She attempted to dart past him, and had almost made it when he caught her by the arm. For a moment she glared at him, then, quicker than thought, she dropped the market basket and her free hand came up in a vigorous slap against that grinning face. Wrenching herself free, she gathered up her skirts and ran, with all the fleetness that had once outstripped every boy at Number Four.

She had marked the place where James had turned, but she reached it too late. The alley was completely empty, and in the moment that she paused to get her bearings, the soldier caught up with her again, a half-dozen delighted boys at his heels. This time there was no breaking away from him. He meant business, and he was quickly reinforced by a fellow soldier at her other elbow.

"Let me go!" Miriam stormed, frantic at missing James. She struggled furiously to free herself, aware, in a panic, that a curious crowd was already hemming her in.

"What is going on here?" The voice was deliberate and authoritative. The crowd gave way before the tall figure that pushed its way through. Looking up, Miriam met the vastly amused gaze of the young *coureur de bois*.

"She was escaping! She is the English prisoner!" the soldier boasted.

"I am not escaping!" Miriam cried. "That's ridiculous! Where could I escape to?"

"You let go of her!" The angry new comment came from Hortense, breathlessly elbowing her way through the spectators. Her indignation had no effect on the soldier.

"She was escaping!" he shouted, twisting her arm tighter. Perhaps he was doing his duty, but certainly he was enjoying it. He had a red mark on his cheek to repay. Suddenly realizing that her violent struggles were only providing a spectacle, Miriam stood still.

"That's enough!" ordered Pierre Laroche. "You have nobly prevented your prisoner from escaping. Now let's hear what she has to say for herself. Let her go, my brave *garçon*."

Miriam shook herself free as the soldiers reluctantly loosened their grip. Now all her frustration was directed toward the *coureur*.

"If people would only mind their own business!" she flared. "I was trying to catch up with Captain Johnson. I saw him go down this street, and I could have caught up with him if only — "

"You could catch up with anyone, that I'll wager," laughed the *coureur*. "*Parbleu!* How you can run! Who are you, anyway?"

Miriam drew herself up. "I am Miriam Willard, Captain Johnson's sister."

"Captain Johnson had an audience with the Governor," broke in the soldier. "He was on his way back to prison. They would all run away if they could."

"I was not running away!"

"She is a stranger," put in Hortense. "She is with Madame Du Quesne, and if you will allow her to come with me —"

"Ah — Madame Du Quesne?" exclaimed Pierre. "Why didn't you say you were a servant of Madame's?"

Miriam's head went still higher. "I am only staying with Madame for a short time while the Captain arranges for our ransom."

"I see. Well, we can easily check your story. We shall ask Madame herself."

Madame! She had entirely forgotten! As the crowd gave way, she saw that the carriage, with its two elegant occupants, still lingered at the street corner. Madame and Felicité must have witnessed this whole undignified affair. In panic and chagrin, Miriam would almost have surrendered herself to the soldier to be dragged off to jail rather than face her mistress before this tittering crowd. But the *coureur* was determinedly leading the way and, propelled by a soldier at each elbow, she had no choice but to follow.

For a moment, as those chill blue eyes looked down from the lofty height of the carriage, Miriam feared

115

that Madame Du Quesne intended not to recognize her at all. But after an interminable inspection the woman spoke.

"Let the girl go, *messieurs*. I am responsible for her. Miriam, what could have possessed you to create such a disgraceful scene?"

"Indeed, I am sorry to embarrass you, Madame. I saw my brother James going down that street."

"That is an odd excuse. Your clothes are torn."

Miriam looked down at her bare shoulder and flushed as she tried to pull together the ripped bodice.

"It is impossible for you to walk home in such a state," said Madame. "I suppose you will have to get into the carriage."

Feeling like a shamed child, Miriam climbed in beside Felicité, shrinking her disheveled self into as small a space as possible to avoid touching those fragrant ruffles.

"You may go about your errands, Hortense," Madame dismissed the anxious girl. "I should have thought I could trust you to take better care of your charge."

Madame gave a command to the driver, and then, as they drove away, remembered to change her stony disapproval to a gracious smile at the young Pierre. In spite of her disgrace, Miriam could not resist a last curious look. The *coureur* was bowing very low, with an elaborate flourish, and by the merest flick of his dancing black eyes, Miriam had the distinct impression that a corner of that flourish was intended for her.

They drove for some time in silence. Felicité said nothing at all, merely gazed at Miriam with round reproachful eyes misted with tears. Miriam felt impelled to speak.

"You must not blame Hortense, Madame," she attempted. "It was entirely my fault, and I know that my sister would be just as shocked as you. It is just that I want so much to know what has happened to the others. Hortense told me that my brother-in-law is in prison, but I saw him turning that corner. Oh, Madame — if you do know where they are, won't you please tell me?"

"If you desired to know about your family, I could have inquired for you," replied Madame. "The members of my household are expected to conduct themselves with propriety. However, what can one expect of the uncivilized English?"

Miriam bit her tongue and kept silent. Not one of the three spoke another word until the house was reached. Then, just as Miriam was hurrying toward the kitchen, she heard a cautious whisper.

"Miriam! Wait!" It was Felicité.

"I think I maybe know something about one of the

117

children. Is there a little girl, about so high, with red curls something like yours, only lighter?"

"Oh, yes! That is Polly. Felicité — do you know where she is?"

"I have seen her," nodded Felicité. "The Mayor's wife has bought her. I didn't think that she might be one of your family."

"But Polly is too little to do any work!"

"Oh, she is not going to work. She is a very lucky girl. You see, the Mayor's wife has never had a baby of her own, and now she is so happy that she has a little English child. She has named her Alphonsine, and she is going to make her a real little French girl."

Miriam was not sure what to think. "Well — if Polly is with someone kind, that is good, of course," she said at last. "But won't this woman feel disappointed when we leave? We shan't be here long, you know?"

"Oh, I don't think she will ever let Polly go," said Felicité doubtfully. "She loves her very much."

James had better hurry, Miriam thought, making her way to the kitchen in a confusion of relief and alarm. Meanwhile she would have to mend her own ways. Felicité at least seemed to have forgiven her, and she was sure that Hortense would bear no ill will. But would Madame ever trust her again?

118

CHAPTER 10

Hortense, as Miriam had trusted, was all sympathy, though she did not conceal that she was also scandalized. It had not been necessary to make such a fuss. Miriam had only to be patient till Jules came tonight with news. True to his word, Jules did bring news. He had learned that Captain Johnson had made a petition which would be considered by the Governor of Canada when he arrived in Montreal. Meanwhile, the Captain was allowed out of the prison only under guard, and was not allowed to communicate with anyone. The two little girls had been purchased by wealthy families. Also, Jules had heard, there was a prisoner by the name of Labaree working on a seigneury north of the city.

Miriam tried to be content with this reassurance. At least they all appeared to be safe. But how drearily the days must drag for Susanna! All she herself could do now was to behave circumspectly and, if it were possible, to win her way back into Madame Du Quesne's good graces.

119

She was astonished, therefore, at an unexpected bit of graciousness on Madame's part. The lady of the house swept into Felicité's room a few mornings later, where Miriam, forgetting her good intentions, was allowing Felicité to chatter aimlessly; was, to be truthful, egging her on. Nothing could have induced her to speak the name of Pierre Laroche, but bit by bit, from Felicité's chance remarks, she was piecing together an intriguing picture. Now, at her mother's step, Felicité hurriedly dipped her pen into the inkpot, and pulled her forehead into exaggerated wrinkles of concern over a neglected sentence.

"Never mind the lesson," said Madame, not at all deceived. "I have word for Miriam. It seems that one of the children — your sister's child did you say? — has been purchased by my good friend the Mayor's wife."

"Thank you, Madame," replied Miriam meekly.

"Now it appears the child is being difficult," Madame went on. "My friend has suggested that I bring you to see her so that perhaps you can reason with her."

"Oh — I should love to see Polly," exclaimed Miriam, delighted and grateful. "I do thank you, Madame."

"I am merely doing it to oblige my friend," Madame assured her. "You will make certain, I trust, that there are no demonstrations this time."

It was too much to expect that there would be no reminders, Miriam thought, flushing. But she must show nothing but gratitude. Felicité was overjoyed.

"Oh, Miriam!" she rejoiced. "Now you will have to go with us in the carriage. What shall I wear, Maman? The new velvet?"

"Certainly not. The blue morning dress will do well enough for this occasion." Madame's gaze lingered deliberately over Miriam — then she shrugged and turned away.

"Be quick," she ordered. "I shall wait for you down-stairs."

The moment the door was closed, Felicité bounced into action. "I've wanted to dress you up ever since you came," she gloated. "Sh! Don't let Maman hear us! Just you wait and see what I'm going to do to you! The blue lustring, I think. It is too small for me anyway."

"But, Madame — !"

"Never mind her. Now, take off that horrid dress!"

The soft lightness of silk slipping over her shoulders gave Miriam a shock of delight.

"You can't look yet," Felicité ordered, fluffing out the full sleeves, tugging at the fastenings. "What a tiny waist you have. I wish mine were as small. I think my foot is smaller than yours, though, but try these shoes anyway. Now — you will need a hat, and gloves. What a pity about your hair — we haven't time to arrange it. But with the hat — see — you tip it just like this. Now! Come and look at yourself!"

Just two steps to the long mirror, but in those two steps Miriam traveled a distance she could never retrace. The girl who looked back from the mirror was a total stranger, yet she had always been there, waiting.

"That is really Miriam Willard!" she said under her breath. She could not drag her eyes away from the vision.

"Come along, silly," urged Felicité. "I think Maman is going to have a fit when she sees you."

Madame was certainly startled. "This was entirely unnecessary." she snapped. For a moment Miriam held her breath, awaiting the order that would strip all the finery away. But Madame shrugged.

"Well, it is late. They are expecting us."

Following Felicité out the front door, teetering in the too tight, high-heeled boots, Miriam felt a heady surge of confidence. She would show these people! Her hat tilted as loftily as Madame's own. This time she would step into that carriage as though she had ridden behind a footman every day of her life!

They had not far to go. In fact they could have walked the distance in a few moments, and the car-

riage had barely set in motion before it drew up at an imposing stone house that Miriam remembered Hortense had pointed out to her on the way to market. What would Hortense think of her now, she wondered, could she see her entering the front door, walking into the drawing room, curtsying to the Mayor's wife, and seating herself delicately on a gilded chair?

Like a punctured bubble her pleasure vanished, when presently a servant led in little Polly. The child's face blurred in the sudden tears that sprang to her eyes. Scrubbed and brushed and dressed in a bright new jumper, Polly looked more sick and miserable than at any time on the Indian trail. She gave no sign that she recognized Miriam, merely stood staring at the strange clothes that had made her aunt an alien like the others.

"Polly dear, 'tis Miriam. Don't you know me?"

Polly refused even to touch her outstretched hand. Were they mistreating the child? She looked so pale and listless. Indignant words sprang to Miriam's lips, but looking up at the Mayor's wife, she could read only bewilderment and concern on that pleasant face.

"Perhaps you can talk to her," the Mayor's wife pleaded. "Tell her to eat her food like a good child. She is so sweet and quiet, no trouble at all except that she will not eat. She needs some good milk and eggs to put roses in her cheeks. Tell me, is there anything she is especially fond of? I will get it for her."

It was impossible to doubt this woman's kind intent. "It is not the food that is wrong," Miriam explained, as tactfully as she could. "Polly has never been away from her mother. Ever since the day we were captured she has needed to have her mother in sight."

There was a sudden cry. Flinging herself violently across the room, Polly buried her head in Miriam's blue skirt.

"Mama!" she wailed. "I want Mama! Take me back to Mama!"

Miriam knelt and hugged the child tight. "Polly, don't cry," she begged. "Mama will come soon.

Please, Polly, be a good girl, so that when Mama comes she will find you looking all pretty and well."

The Mayor's wife reached down and dragged Polly away, holding her firmly on her own lap. "I did not ask you to come here to lie to the child," she accused Miriam.

"Lie to her?"

"It will do no good to deceive her," the woman repeated. "Alphonsine has a new mother now. She must learn to be a good little French girl."

"But, madame —"

"You have done nothing but upset her. She has never cried like this before. Please go now, quickly."

Madame Du Quesne was only too ready to end this distressing affair. As Polly was borne howling from the room, she maneuvered the girls through the door, and into the carriage, with the bitter wails echoing in their ears.

So Miriam was not a grand lady, fashionably dressed, making a morning call in a genteel manner. The pretty picture was shattered. No matter how dressed-up they might be, she and Polly were prisoners.

Madame Du Quesne surprisingly showed a moment's sympathy. "She will not cry long," she said, briskly. "She will be quite all right as soon as you are out of sight, and some day she will come to realize what a fortunate little girl she is. Now, since you are out with us, I think I shall take you to call on the other child, and you will see how foolish your suspicions have been."

It was a considerably humbled girl who alighted at the next door. This house was nowhere near so grand. It was an older, one-story wooden dwelling with a scarlet-painted door. The room into which they stepped was cozy and welcoming. Miriam looked about for Susanna with apprehension, and could hardly believe her eyes when the child came running joyously to meet her.

"What a pretty dress!" Sue cried. "Miriam, you look just beautiful!"

Miriam seized the child's hands and smiled back at her affectionately. Sue had been eating, beyond a doubt. Her cheeks were round and pink, and her chubby little legs showed sturdily under the short dress.

"You look beautiful too," Miriam answered. "You've grown an inch, Sue, and you look so — so grown up."

"It's my new shoes. I just got them yesterday." Sue held out a foot for Miriam to admire, clad in a dainty white-topped leather boot that Felicité might envy.

"I have a red pair, too, to wear to school every day, and I have six white petticoats. I have a room all to myself with a big bed. Come and see where I sleep Miriam."

Miriam looked up at the two women who stood behind Sue. One was tall and sharp-nosed, with gray in her hair; the other was younger and rounder, but both had exactly the same expression of fond pride and pleasure.

"She wants to show me her room," Miriam interpreted, and the two women smiled more broadly than before. Excusing herself from Madame Du Quesne, Miriam allowed Sue to pull her through the curtained doorway, through a tidy chamber where the two women apparently slept, into a tiny bedroom beyond. This room was so new and pretty, so recently painted and freshly curtained that it must have been expressly planned for the little girl who slept there.

"What a lovely room, Sue," Miriam said admiringly. "But I thought you were at a convent."

"I was, for quite a few days. It was nice there too. But then *Tante* Claudine and *Tante* Anne came to get me. They said I would be their little girl. Tante Anne made all these clothes for me. I like her better than Tante Claudine. She plays little games with me so I can understand what she says."

"Where do you go to school?"

"At the Convent. Tante Anne takes me there every morning. Miriam, there are Indian girls there too, and

they dress just like us. They aren't like the Indians at
Saint Francis. They can sew so fast, much faster than
I can."

"Are you really learning to sew?"

"Look what I'm making, Miriam. 'Tis an etui."

Miriam admired the little bag with its bright blue
embroidery.

"I'm making it for Mama. Do you think she will
like it?"

Underneath all the chatter and vanity Sue was still
a little girl who missed her mother.

"Mama will love it," Miriam said. "You must hurry
and finish it before she comes."

"When is she coming, Miriam?"

"I don't know, dear. I wish she could know how
safe and well you are here."

Sue looked down at her new boots thoughtfully.
"I wish Polly could be here too. Do you know where
Polly is, Miriam? Does she have a nice room to sleep
in?"

"I've just been to see Polly. She has pretty clothes
just like you, but she isn't happy. You know how she
always wanted to be near her mama."

Sue's face was sober. "Poor Polly. She's too little
to know about the Blessed Mother."

Miriam started. "What do you mean, Sue?"

"See, up there? The sisters gave it to me. She takes
care of me."

Miriam was disturbed. Indeed she had noticed, the moment she had entered the room, the little statue that hung above Susanna's bed. What heathenish things were these women teaching a four-year-old child who could not understand any better?

"What have they told you, Sue?" There was a fierceness in her tone that brought sudden tears to the child's eyes.

"They said she is the mother of our Lord," she explained, her lips trembling. "They said I must pray to her every night to keep Mama and the baby safe out there in the woods. Isn't it all right for me to, Miriam?"

It was all wrong, Miriam knew. All her life she had been taught to despise this mysterious evil called Popery. Her grandfather had left England so that his children would never be taught such things. But looking down into Susanna's troubled face, Miriam did not know what to say. She looked back instead at the little statue of the mother and child. It was a simple hand-carved figure, but it had been fashioned with skill and reverence. There was such gentleness in the way the mother's arm curved about her child.

"Don't you think she's pretty?" Sue asked. "Mama used to sit beside the fire and rock Captive just like that. In the night when I wake up and it's all dark, I reach up and touch her, and then I can go back to sleep."

Miriam stooped and put both arms around Susanna. "I think she's beautiful," she whispered. "I'm sure it can't be wrong, Sue, if it keeps you from being lonely. When Mama comes you can tell her about it."

The puckers smoothed out of Sue's forehead. She wiped her eyes on the corner of Miriam's kerchief and was her practical little self again. "I hope she comes soon," she said confidently. "I want to show her my new shoes. Do you think when I go with Mama they will let me keep them?"

That night, lying awake in the darkness of the loft over the kitchen, Miriam's troubled thoughts went back to those disturbing moments. What should she have answered? Sue's childish question had confronted her with a puzzle she had been trying to thrust into a far corner of her mind. What was there that was so dreadful about the way these people worshiped? At home everyone had spoken of the French as an idolatrous folk. But surely Hortense and Felicité, the kind women she had met today, even Madame, for all her haughtiness, were not wicked. Moreover, she could not escape seeing, as she went about the city, that their religion was as real and natural a part of these people's lives as the air and sunshine. On the streets the gentle priests and sisters mingled with the common folk and were greeted as friends.

Last Sunday morning Hortense had offered to take

130

her to church but, terrified at the thought, she had sat alone in the kitchen and repeated every word she could remember of the Divine Service. In the wilderness James had never allowed them to omit their worship. It was up to her now to uphold that faith. Yet today, confronted by Sue's troubled eyes, she had betrayed all her teaching.

Her own father would be angry, she knew. Susanna? She was not sure. There was a stern core of duty in Susanna that would make it difficult to ask her such a question. There was one person she longed to ask. Phineas Whitney, who was planning to become a minister. Strange, when they had never had the slightest chance to speak of such things, that she knew she would never be afraid to ask him anything.

She was glad she had answered as she had. Somehow, no matter what Susanna might say, she could not believe that a difference in belief should cause any child to be lonely and afraid. It was a very new thought.

CHAPTER II

Early in November bleak weather settled over the city, and the sky was heavy with the threat of early snow. Looking up at the lowering black rock, Miriam shivered. How would Susanna make out, in a flimsy wigwam? In a short time the river would be frozen, and the winter snows would seal off the village of St. Francis for months to come. How could she bear the coming winter with no word from Susanna?

"Madame wishes to see you in the drawing room," announced one of the maids one noonday, coming into the kitchen where Miriam and Hortense were peeling mushrooms for the evening casserole. Miriam smoothed a quick hand over her hair and apron. Doubtless there was some special service that Madame required. The morning drive was already over, and even so she had lost hope that that extraordinary invitation would ever be repeated. Now she was startled as she entered the drawing room to see that Madame had guests, a rather shabbily dressed lady and a gen-

132

tleman in a gray coat.

"Come in, my dear," Madame greeted her, in so warm and indulgent a tone that Miriam faltered in the doorway. Then the strangers turned toward her.

"Susanna!" Miriam cried, forgetting as usual all decorum and flinging herself across the room toward her sister. "Susanna dear! Is it actually you?"

It was truly Susanna, in a French silk dress. She was thinner than ever; there were hollows under her cheek bones, but her eyes were brilliant with happiness, for the gentleman in the gray coat was James.

"I shall leave you to visit with your sister," Madame announced. "I know how happy you both must be."

"What in the world has come over Madame?" Miriam marveled, and then forgot that contradictory lady in a new astonishment. At Susanna's feet, in a wicker basket, lay an incredible little doll. It was Captive, dressed like a French baby, her small face peering incongruously out from a mass of white ruffles and lace.

"She does look comical, doesn't she?" Susanna smiled. "I scarcely recognized her myself. When the Indians left us at the French fort the officers' wives dressed her like a French baby. They gave me this handsome dress to wear, too."

"Sylvanus?" Miriam was sorry she had asked, as the shadow fell across Susanna's face.

"He did not come back from the hunt. They have taken him to some other village. I could not even find out where."

"The little girls are fine, though," Miriam hurried to assure her.

"I know. I saw them both this morning. Sue is quite content. I'm sure those good women are spoiling her. But Polly — oh dear, she did nothing but cry. The

French lady forbade me to come again. Think of it, Miriam, my own baby! But we must be patient a little longer. James will straighten everything out soon."

"It has taken much longer than I expected," James explained."At first no one would listen to me. But finally the Governor has agreed to allow me two months on parole and I am starting out for Albany to-day. Once there I can go on to Boston to obtain money to redeem all of us. In the meantime, Monsieur Du Quesne has agreed to care for you both during my absence, and he will be well recompensed on my return."

"I am afraid they have not allowed nearly enough time for such a journey," Susanna put in anxiously.

"The snow has not yet begun," James answered, "and the hard ground should make it easy to travel. I am quite certain there will be no trouble. I have given my bond that I shall return with the money within two months."

"Do they trust you to go alone, just on your promise?"

"There will be two Mohawks sent to keep an eye on me. But the rank of Captain carries some weight in this city. In fact, the Governor has made them understand that we are prisoners of considerable importance. He has ordered Monsieur Du Quesne to treat you as his guests, not as prisoners, and I have

135

guaranteed that his kindness will be amply repaid. I understand you have been living here as a servant, Miriam. That is to be changed from now on."

How incredibly it was all to be changed Miriam soon discovered. Madame Du Quesne, obviously chagrined that she had failed to recognize in the English girl a prisoner of importance, now outdid herself to be affable. Under promise of repayment her generosity flowered. Miriam was whisked from the kitchen and from the loft mattress she had shared with Hortense and installed with Susanna in a guest chamber with a fine canopied bed. Madame's wardrobe and Felicité's were ransacked to provide a collection of hand-me-downs. There was no more cleaning or polishing and cooking. Miriam now sat with the family at the long dining-room table, with its white cloth, its crystal goblets and silver candlesticks. She could never manage to be at ease there, however, and her tongue was completely tied between the remote politeness of Monsieur Du Quesne at one end and the critical supervision of his wife at the other.

Felicité had her way now, and the lessons, which Miriam tried to continue, dwindled to a mere pretense, interrupted by an endless discussion of where they would be going, what they would wear.

"Do you think the green damask?" Felicité would ponder, "or the pink lustring? If I wear the pink you

136

must wear your purple. It becomes you so well."

"You mean it sets off your pink costume so perfectly," Miriam would tease.

"Oh, Miriam, you are so droll! Of course, it does go with the pink, but really it makes you look sweet. Do wear it, Miriam!"

Miriam would wear the purple dress, which actually made her look sallow, because it was fun to please Felicité, and exciting to be included in the plans regardless of the dress Felicité chose. More than that, it was intoxicating beyond belief to have this charming lighthearted girl for a real friend at last.

Miriam was initiated now into the life that had seemed so mysterious viewed from the kitchen. Mainly it consisted of a succession of formal calls for which half the morning was spent in elaborate preparation. The right gown had to be chosen, the hair curled and dressed, every detail exhaustively considered. Then the carriage would draw up at the door to take them the short distance to one of the tall stone houses where other ladies, having finished the same careful toilette, greeted them. Sometimes the hours were enlivened by gossip and card games. After a little private instruction from Felicité, Miriam took courage to defy her sister Susanna, who frowned on card playing, and discovered that the games were more satisfying to her lively spirits than the endless conversations.

137

Evenings, however, to which the whole day seemed a prelude, still remained a mystery. Occasionally Miriam and Susanna were invited to dine with the Du Quesnes at one of the grand mansions on the hill. More often they sat quietly in the guest chamber while Felicité departed in a flurry of rustling fragrance to dancing parties, or sleighrides on the frozen river. Felicité had so many admirers. They were constantly sending her graceful notes and pretty trinkets, and her invitations were piled up for weeks ahead. Of all these beaux, Miriam knew that Pierre Laroche created the nearest approach to a flutter in Felicité's capricious heart. She had glimpsed, once or twice, his bold laughing face in the doorway, but always she shrank hastily out of sight lest he should recognize her. Someday, Felicité promised, they must find a young man who would invite Miriam to these evening affairs. She seemed in no great hurry to find him, however, and, truthfully, the English colonist from Charlestown was a little terrified at the idea.

The weeks sped by. The snow, which had begun in late November, drifted ever deeper in the narrow streets. The frozen stretches of the St. Lawrence became a vast white wasteland. By Christmastide the white blanket reached as high as the windows. Little Susanna, clinging to Tante Anne's hand, came to call, snug in a trim coat and cap and muff of delicate white fur. January came and went, and February. There were days when it was impossible to leave the house, and Felicité and Miriam whiled away the hours with embroidery and cards. Then a path would be cleared once more in the street, and friends would gather again, all the gayer for the brief separation.

Thrilling as all this was to Miriam, it left Susanna untouched. Charming and witty Susanna could be when she chose, and she dutifully roused herself to repay the generosity of these new friends. For the most part she was abstracted, and her eyes were shadowed. It had been hard to part with James again when they had scarcely been reunited, and the journey to New England in winter through Indian territory was hazardous. There was still no word of Sylvanus, the apple of her eye, and her two daughters were estranged from her in their French homes. Only Captive, gaining rapidly on good provincial bread and milk, could coax a real warmth into her eyes.

She barely lifted an eyebrow the morning that Miriam came rushing into the room so enraptured she could scarcely speak.

"We are going to a ball, Susanna! Think of it! The most important ball of the whole season, and Felicité has coaxed her mother into taking us!"

" 'Tis very kind of them," murmured Susanna, not raising her head from the page she was writing.

"Susanna! Listen to me!" demanded Miriam, seizing the pen from her sister's hand. "Stop writing those letters all the time. James will be back before you find anyone to carry them for you. Why can't you enjoy life while we are here?"

Susanna studied Miriam's flushed, impatient face. " 'Tis very important to you, isn't it?" she asked thoughtfully. "All this dressing up, and the dinners and the ball."

"Why shouldn't it be?"

"I can't feel that 'tis real," Susanna warned. "These people have too much idle time on their hands, and they seize anything to divert themselves. We are just a novelty, a sort of outlandish amusement."

"That's unfair! I know Felicité likes me. Do you have to be stiff and suspicious? Why, we could have lived our whole lives and never even heard of a ball. When we go back we'll never as long as we live have another chance. Please, Susanna, don't be solemn and spoil it all!"

"Very well," agreed Susanna, smiling in spite of herself. "We shall go to this wonderful ball. And what do we wear?"

"They will give us something. Felicité is having a new gown made. She's been describing it for days."

Nothing else was talked about in the blue and white bedroom. Felicité had found the most flattering audience imaginable for her constant prattle. Miriam drank in every detail of the great event to come. She knew what each of their friends would wear, which of the young men would likely pay attention to which girl.

"Of course," said Felicité, "lots of the nicest men have already gone on their silly trading. I can't imagine why they should want to go out in the woods when they could have such fun here. But Pierre will be here. He has promised not to leave."

Promised whom? Felicité herself, Miriam surmised, noting the way the French girl glanced from under her lashes toward the mirror at the mention of his name. Miriam felt a prick of envy. Even more wonderful than looking forward to a ball must be the certainty of knowing that a special young man would be waiting there. Just suppose she could know that Phineas Whitney — ? But how ridiculous! Phineas was a million miles away, and he probably would not know how to behave at a grand affair like this. She sprang to her feet and shook off the memory.

"Show me again how to do the minuet," she begged. "I always forget how to do the turn."

Not until two days before the ball did Madame Du Quesne remember to provide her two guests with something to wear. Miriam wondered if she would have remembered then without Felicité's constant prodding. At last, after a lengthy conference behind

141

Felicité's closed door, she came to the guest chamber with two gowns and laid them graciously across the big bed. Miriam pounced before Madame's back was fairly turned, but Susanna touched the folds reluctantly, her forehead perplexed.

"It doesn't seem right," she said. "Such costly gowns as these. James can never bring back enough money to pay for such things."

"Don't be silly, Susanna. Madame won't expect to be paid for these. She and Felicité are all through with them. Besides, she doesn't want us to disgrace her."

"You should not speak like that about Madame," Susanna rebuked her, not for the first time. "She has been very generous to us both."

Miriam refused to be impressed with Madame's generosity. Now that she had had a good look at these dresses she felt miserably disappointed. She was no longer the naïve colonist she had been three months before. In their morning calls she and Felicité had often been spirited away by their young friends for a little unrestrained gossip upstairs. They had spent many a delightful hour going through each other's closets and taking surreptitious peeks into their elders' wardrobes as well.

"These dresses aren't so wonderful as you think," Miriam said now, with her recently gained knowledge.

142

"The material is fine, but they are all out of style. The ladies just aren't wearing sleeves like this, and the new dresses all have pleats in the back."

Susanna was amused. "Since when have you been an authority on French dressmaking?"

"I use my eyes," Miriam answered, seeing nothing amusing. "As a matter of fact, I could show these French dressmakers a thing or two. They just copy the one or two styles that come over from Paris. They dress everyone alike — the short fat women and the tall thin ones. Look at this now, it would make you look like a pincushion!"

With a gasp of horror, Susanna saw Miriam's scissors slash ruthlessly through the expensive satin. "Miriam! How dare you! You have ruined it!"

"Wait and see," predicted Miriam. "There! We can cut it away here to show the lace petticoat, and have material enough to make gathers in the back."

All day long and half the night Miriam snipped and stitched, tried on and ripped out and stitched again, until the one candle in the room sputtered out and forced her to shut her smarting eyes.

"I don't know how you do it," her sister worried. "If I took out one of those seams I could never get it together again. How could you know this would look so well?"

"The thing is, I care and you really don't," said

143

Miriam. "I wager you'd have worn your old brown homespun."

" 'Twould have seemed more fitting," Susanna agreed, quite unruffled. "This grand lady you've made me into isn't I at all. I doubt James would approve. 'Tis scandalous low."

"James would just about burst with pride if he could see you, I know he would. Now stand still. This panel has to be shortened. And then you've got to fit my waist in tighter. I can't reach behind my back."

Even Susanna was impressed when Miriam tried on her yellow satin gown. The heavy shining silk molded her slim waist snugly in front, and fell back to reveal a handsome petticoat made from the salvaged portions of a frayed summer dress. In the back the material was gathered in three stylish Watteau pleats, smoothed flat to the waist, and flaring below. Sitting back on her heels, Susanna stared.

"I declare, Miriam, you do have a knack! I don't believe there's a lovelier gown in Boston, or even in Paris!"

To Felicité Miriam had given no inkling of what was going on; but, unable to wait another moment to display her creation, she intercepted Hortense on the way downstairs and drew her into the room, her finger on her lips. She had seen very little of Hortense all these weeks. It was like old times to share a secret with her again.

144

She could not have asked for a more satisfying audience. As she revolved slowly in the new dress, the French girl oh'd and ah'd, her black eyes dancing, her round face wrinkled with pleasure. Hortense, friendly and matter of fact, seemed not in the least overawed by Miriam's new status, or even conscious that she herself had been neglected. But once or twice as they talked, Miriam noticed a fleeting twinkle in her old friend's eye that brought an instant's discomfort. Could Hortense possibly be laughing at her? She checked herself, all at once aware that she had been prattling exactly like Felicité. Well, was that so amusing? If Hortense had any idea how starved she had been all her life for companionship she would not begrudge her a little fun now.

Indeed, Hortense herself said as much. "I'm so glad you are having a good time, Miriam. You do deserve it after all you have been through." Then, revealing that she was only human after all, a small touch of envy crept into Hortense's voice.

"You look so lovely in that dress, Miriam," she said wistfully. "I wish that just once in my life, just for my wedding, I could have a beautiful dress. But isn't that silly? Where would I ever wear it when the wedding was over? To milk the cows?"

CHAPTER 12

Hours before the dance Felicité came in search of Miriam. "Come," she ordered. "Lucille is to dress my hair now, and while it is being done one of the other maids can do yours too. Maman says it is not necessary, but she needn't know till it is all done."

"You mean — powdered?" asked Miriam doubtfully.

"Of course. Every lady there will have her hair powdered. And I'll give you some cream and powder for your face, and a tiny beauty spot to put right there." Felicité's silvery laugh broke out at Miriam's uncertainty. "What are you afraid of, silly? We will make you look just beautiful."

"Can Hortense be the one to help me?"

"Hortense? But she is a little simpleton, a habitant! What would she know about doing hair? Maman's maids were trained in Paris. Come — we can watch each other in the mirror."

So Miriam sat for the first time for the elaborate toilette she had often watched Felicité undergo. It

146

was more torture than delight. Seemingly for hours she held her head rigid and followed in the mirror the deft fingers of the maid. The curling iron hissed and steamed, as the heavy red hair was massed high on her head in countless curls and twists. Miriam's back and neck ached long before the intricate creation was finished to Felicité's satisfaction. Then the maid brought the quail pipe, and Miriam covered her eyes while the white powder was blown into the red curls. Finally there was perfumed cream for her cheeks, powder, and a touch of rouge, and the little black beauty spot, which Felicité herself insisted on pasting just beneath her left eye.

When Miriam returned to her room Susanna was already dressed, sitting at the desk writing the daily letter that would never reach James as though this were any ordinary evening. The startled eyes she lifted to Miriam were disconcerting.

"Felicité says to come quickly," Miriam hurried to say. "There is still time to fix your hair too."

"Thank you," answered Susanna. "My hair is already done." It lay against her head in two smooth dark wings, and was coiled in a neat bun at the back of her neck.

"You can't leave it like that!" Miriam's exasperation flared. "After I worked so hard! You won't look like the others."

Susanna stood up from the desk slowly. "I am not like the others," she said quietly. "I am an Englishwoman. I have done my hair like this all my life, and I have no intention of doing it any differently."

The rebuke in Susanna's voice was too much for Miriam to bear. Furious tears threatened the powder and rouge. "Oh go ahead then," she stormed "Look like a — a habitant! 'Tis all right for you to throw away your chances. But I'm young, and I know what I want!"

"What do you want?"

"I want to be a part of life, not forever waiting and looking on at other people. I want to wear clothes that I can be proud of. And I want — oh stop hatcheling me! It is almost time to go and I have to get my dress on."

Susanna started to reply and then abruptly changed her mind. She stepped forward and silently eased Miriam's dress off her shoulders so as not to disturb the glistening structure. Miriam, somewhat mollified, accepted the gesture as a peace offering. There was no time now for argument or even for thinking. Susanna held the yellow gown for Miriam to step into, and bent to adjust the intricate fastenings. Then she stepped back to inspect her younger sister.

"Of course, they say the English ladies in Boston powder their hair," she conceded. "You are a picture,

Miriam. I declare, you take my breath away."

Miriam felt a rush of gratitude. "Don't mind the things I said, Susanna," she returned generously. "You look beautiful, really, just the way you are." And all at once, looking at her sister in the perfectly fitting red silk, Miriam realized that it was actually true. What was there about Susanna that, standing there so plain and severe, without knowing or caring, she had a beauty not one of them could touch? For an instant a hint of misgiving quivered in Miriam's mind. She whirled anxiously to the mirror and there found the reassurance she needed. Yes, the girl in the mirror was everything she had ever dreamed or longed for. The dreams that had begun that October morning in Felicité's borrowed gown had all come true at last.

"They will be waiting for us," she murmured, embarrassed lest Susanna read her mind. So the two Willard sisters, each unshaken in her own choice but united once more in affection, linked arms and went down the stairs together.

Felicité was standing in the middle of the hall, a pink and white confection. Even more flattering than the mirror was the astonishment that rounded the little red Cupid's bow of her lips.

"Meeriam! Your dress! What did you do to it? Isn't it beautiful, Maman? Would you ever dream it was my last year's second-best?"

149

Madame did not bother to answer. Ice-blue eyes narrowed, she studied the two English women, taking in every detail, dwelling thoughtfully on the folds that had been gathered so carefully to reveal Miriam's neck and shoulders. Finally she turned to her daughter.

"I forgot something, Felicité," she said airily. "You look a little plain in that dress. I think you may wear the necklace tonight."

"Maman! Grandmère's necklace?" With a torrent of endearments Felicité threw herself at her mother in an ecstatic embrace that threatened to undo all the labor of the Parisian maid. Madame gave her an impatient push. The necklace was brought, lifted reverently from its blue velvet box, and fastened about the girl's plump white throat. Felicité, who had looked anything but plain before, was now positively dazzling. Miriam gasped. Conscious of her own bare throat and arms, she glanced at Susanna. Her sister's lips twitched ever so slightly, and in Susanna's dark eyes Miriam surprised a gleam of something that was certainly not envy.

From the moment they left the carriage and stepped out of the snowy street into the brilliantly lighted ballroom of the Governor's mansion, Miriam drifted in a dream world, apart from any reality she had ever known. Under crystal chandeliers ablaze with candles, across a shining floor boarded by velvet hangings,

dream figures wheeled to the heart-catching music of violins. Women in flower-like satins and frothy lace rested their hands delicately on gold-braided shoulders. The very air she breathed was perfumed and intoxicating.

Nothing that happened in this dream world was improbable. It was not unbelievable that Monsieur Du Quesne, who had barely nodded good morning for weeks, should bow low to kiss Susanna's hand and then her own, nor that strange young men should click their heels and offer their arms for one dance after another. It seemed altogether natural that her feet should move of their own volition in the steps that Felicité had coached.

That she herself, so intriguingly different from the others, so blazingly alive and radiant, was a phenomenon in this place, she did not stop to reason. The admiration made her lightheaded, as though she had tasted the wine Susanna had forbidden her to touch. She forgot Felicité and Madame Du Quesne, forgot that these people were enemies and that she was a prisoner. She even forgot Susanna, who, refusing to dance, was still surrounded in spite of herself by a small court of admirers.

She could not even be surprised when she tilted back her head as an especially tall young man was presented, and looked straight into the bold black eyes she had never forgotten.

He cannot possibly recognize me now, she thought, preening herself as his arm encircled her waist and they moved across the floor. But Pierre Laroche's first words were shattering.

"I see the girl who can run like an Indian can dance as well," he said, and laughed to see the blood rush into her cheeks.

152

"I can't fancy what you can be talking about," Miriam attempted, in Madame's best manner.

"Oh yes you can," he chuckled. "You were not so high and mighty when you tore into that soldier like a little wildcat."

"'Tis unfair of you to remember that," Miriam protested. "I am not in the least that sort of person actually."

"No? They are changing you fast, I can see that. What a pity about your hair. A crime to put out those lovely flames with a mess of powder." His fingers rested lightly against the white curls.

Miriam did not know how to deal with such conversation. "How do you come to be here?" she asked hurriedly. "They said you were a *coureur de bois.*"

"So you inquired about me?"

"I — I remember that someone spoke of it. I thought that all the *coureurs* were gone in the winter."

"Take a good look at me. Do I look like a *coureur?* You have failed to notice my new uniform."

Indeed, now that she ventured to look straight at him, she recognized the white coat with its brilliant facings and the gold insignia of an officer.

"I have joined the forces of His Majesty. For one year only. I am no soldier, you understand. King Louis is welcome to settle his wars without me. But when the English interfere with my business, that is another matter."

He ignored the stiffening of the yellow-satin back against his hand.

"My mother, bless her soul, thinks I am prepared to settle down at last and be a gentleman, but she is mistaken. No honest *coureur* can stay harnessed for long. One year I have promised her, till we get rid of the English who are moving in on our good beaver land."

"What makes you so sure you can accomplish that in one year?" Miriam could not resist scoffing.

"Ha! Less than that perhaps! Do you think any French soldier is not a match for at least three Eng-

154

lishmen? And when the *coureurs de bois* lend a hand
— poof! The war is as good as over!"

"You take a great deal for granted. You may get a
surprise," said Miriam, her temper rising.

"But who is to surprise us? A handful of yokels who
don't even have uniforms to wear? It will be like going
out to flush an army of woodchucks."

"How dare you!" Miriam flashed, her pride finally
stung out of hiding. "Let me go at once! I will not
listen to such talk!"

Pierre threw back his head and laughed so boister-
ously that other dancers turned their heads to stare.

"*Tiens!*" he conceded. "No doubt the English are
heroes to a man. I merely wanted to see behind that
disguise of yours. There is plenty of wildcat still left.
Now that I'm sure of it you need not have your eye on
any more partners. Now you will have supper with
me. Uniform or not, I am still a *coureur,* and I enjoy eating with savages."

CHAPTER 13

THE HOUSE was very quiet next morning when Miriam made her way to Felicité's room. It was almost noon. Even allowing for the scandalous hour they had come in, Felicité could not possibly still be asleep. The silence of the hall, however, encouraged the uneasy doubts that had been nibbling at the edge of her pleasure. It reminded her of the utter silence in which the four women had ridden home last night, a silence which at the time she had been far too enraptured to heed. She knocked on Felicité's door, and then, as always, opened it and peeked inside.

"Go away!" ordered Felicité. "I have a headache. I don't want to see anyone."

Miriam shut the door. Across the hallway Hortense, with an untouched breakfast tray, was just emerging from Madame's chamber, and from the twinkle in her eye Miriam saw that she had overheard.

"Mademoiselle is out of sorts this morning?" whispered Hortense. "Are you surprised?"

Miriam did not answer. She wanted to stay wrapped in her rosy dream. But even more she wanted to talk to someone, so she tiptoed down the stairs after Hortense, through the quiet rooms, into the familiar kitchen.

"Why shouldn't I be surprised?" she demanded, when it was safe to speak out loud.

"Oh, stop pretending, Miriam. Sometimes lately you sound just like Felicité. Did you think we would not all know how Madame is very angry?"

"She did act queerly last night," Miriam admitted. "I guess I wasn't paying much attention."

"Maybe you should pay attention. Lucille, she helped Madame undress last night, and she told us the whole thing. Such a to-do! Madame, she was raging at everyone. She even slapped Lucille for breaking a drawstring. She swore she'd send you and your sister back to the Indians this morning. Felicité was crying her pretty eyes out. Monsieur, he finally got them quieted down. But Lucille said Madame would surely like to scratch your eyes out!"

"But why, Hortense? Madame invited us. She gave us the dresses. Was it wrong that I had a good time? Did she expect that no one would dance with me?"

"She never expected what happened, that's certain. According to her, you made eyes at every man there. And those old gowns you fixed up so they looked bet-

157

ter than their brand-new ones. Madame says you did it on purpose, to humiliate her."

"The idea! I did no such thing!"

"No? Don't glare at me. I am just telling you what I heard. Madame said you put on airs like the Queen of France. Miriam, you know what is really the matter. You think we have not heard that too? You think we don't know about that handsome Pierre Laroche?"

"Maybe you know more than I do," Miriam answered crossly. "Go ahead, what did they say?"

"Felicité said he danced with you seven times. And when he was dancing with the others he looked at you and didn't hear what anyone said. You think Felicité would like that?"

"But Felicité has so many beaux! What difference would just one make? Do you think she is in love with him, Hortense?"

"Oh — love!" Hortense shrugged her shoulders. "What would Felicité know about love? It is Madame. Pierre Laroche — so rich, so handsome! All the mamans have an eye on Pierre for a long time. You think they would enjoy it that an English girl walks off with him right under their noses?"

"I didn't walk off with him! He just kept coming back. He — oh Hortense, everything happened so fast. It was so exciting. I never stopped to think. Oh dear! If I spoiled the party for Felicité, I'm sorry."

"Very sorry?" prodded Hortense, with such a shrewd twinkle that Miriam had to laugh. Suddenly, looking at each other, both girls were overtaken by helpless giggles, just as in the early days together. They clung to each other, weak with laughter.

"All the same, I'm scared now," said Miriam finally, wiping her eyes. "What do you think I ought to do? Apologize to Madame?"

"I think you should stay well out of Madame's way for a day or two."

"May I stay down here with you?"

Hortense clapped a hand over her mouth. *"Peste!* I forgot Madame wanted an ice pack for her forehead. Come back later, Miriam. If you like, we can walk to the baker's together."

Miriam was still suppressing a giggle as she climbed the stairs to her own chamber. Though her conscience did prick her, the joke was too delicious not to relish. She hurried to pour out every detail to a sober Susanna, who found nothing amusing in the recital.

" 'Tis very unfortunate," Susanna shook her head. "I should never have consented to our going. This is a shameful way to have repaid Madame's kindness."

"Don't preach, Susanna. Madame hasn't a drop of kindness in her, and you know it. She treats us as though we were Indians. All that generosity is only a pose before her friends. If it weren't for James's

159

agreement with Monsieur you'd have been put to work in the kitchen the way I was."

"'Twould have been more fitting than all this foolishness."

"You needn't sound so righteous. You enjoyed it as much as I did. Every time I looked at you last night you were having the time of your life."

Susanna flushed. "I admit, I did enjoy it," she confessed. "I'm shamed to think of it now. I'm not blaming you, Miriam. You're young and it was all new to you. But that I should have forgotten myself, and with James gone so long!" Susanna buried her face in her hands.

"You can't blame yourself either. You didn't even dance. All you did was forget to act solemn for once. Besides, no one would have minded, if it hadn't been for Pierre."

Susanna raised her head. "That young *coureur*, Miriam — you wouldn't — I mean — a trader like that. He's not a proper person at all."

Miriam laughed. "You don't need to worry. Madame will make sure I never lay eyes on him again. But you must admit, it was exciting."

Susanna shook her head. "'Twas not worth it. Besides, there is more to this than just what happened last night. I've been expecting trouble for weeks. James has been gone too long."

"We knew he could not make it in two months. They could not expect it. I'm sure he's all right, Susanna."

"I pray so. I make myself believe that he is. But will these French people be patient? I suppose we can only go on waiting."

Waiting was a task poorly suited to Miriam's nature. For the next three days Felicité sulked in her room, tripped haughtily past on the way to the door, and refused to meet Miriam's eye at the dinner table. Madame also behaved as though the two English women were invisible. When the hours dragged in the quiet bedchamber, Miriam went in search of Hortense.

Early the fourth afternoon a servant knocked at the door with word that Madame Johnson was to come to the drawing room at once.

"Shall I go with you?" Miriam asked. "'Tis not fair for you to have to face Madame all alone."

"There was no mention of you. Never fear, I am quite capable of facing Madame by myself."

"No doubt of that," Miriam admitted. "You're a match for a dozen of her any day. But I'm sorry you have to suffer for what I've done, truly I am."

As the minutes dragged by Miriam would far rather have been with Susanna facing the most blasting storm than waiting in this quiet room. What could be taking so long? Captive, as though she sensed that something was amiss, was unusually peevish. More than an hour had passed before the door opened and Susanna came slowly into the room, dropped into a chair, and covered her face with her hands.

"What is it?" Miriam demanded. "Tell me — what could they have said to you?"

"We are to leave this house," Susanna said painfully. "They will not have us here another night."

"Why, Susanna? Just because of those silly dresses?"

"No. I told you that was only part of it. They think James has broken his bond. The two Indians came back a week ago. They say they left James in Albany early in December, and he was well and strong. Thank God for that at least! He had to go on to Boston to get the money. They waited seven weeks, but he never came back. Monsieur Du Quesne says he never intended to come back, that it was all just a trick to get his freedom. My James, who never broke his word to anyone in his life!"

"Do you think he could not get the money?"

"Other families have been redeemed. Perhaps he fell ill. Perhaps he is even — "

"Susanna! That is not like you at all! I am sure he is on the way, right now."

"The Indians reported there is fighting breaking out

162

everywhere. I doubt he could get through now."

"James will get through somehow. You know he will. They just *have* to give us more time."

"The time has run out. I pleaded with him, Miriam, as though I had no pride at all, and he would not even listen."

" 'Tis Madame who's behind it, the hateful thing! I know she has nagged him into it."

"Perhaps. But there is the money too. They didn't take us in out of charity, remember. You have always forgotten that we were prisoners."

Miriam thought for a moment. There was a solution, and she must face it, without even letting Susanna know how much it would cost.

"We can work here," she managed to say. "We can be servants the way I was before you came."

Susanna dismissed this heroic gesture. "I asked him that too. They will not have us in the house. That much at least is the other night's doing."

Tears rolled down Miriam's cheeks. "It is all my fault then. I knew it."

Susanna reached a comforting hand. "Don't take on, Miriam. I have wondered how long they would keep us. Now, help me get ready before they find us still here."

"But — how can we carry things out?"

"I shall take nothing," said Susanna, "except the

dress they gave me at the fort that first day. That was given me freely without thought of any return. Nor shall you, Miriam. That homespun dress you had on the day I came here will be sufficient."

"That plain old thing? You can't mean it! Why, that's what the habitants wear."

Susanna turned a stern eye. "And what are we, better than habitants? They are self-respecting people like our neighbors at home."

"But all those beautiful things! I can't leave them behind. No one wants them."

"They were loaned to you, not given. Monsieur Du Quesne said outright that we already owe him more than we could hope to repay in years. Miriam, he even threatened to put us in jail as debtors."

"He wouldn't dare! He only said that to scare you."

"He meant it! I'm so afraid of the jail, Miriam. Better if we'd never left Saint Francis."

Miriam's defiance crumpled. She climbed glumly into the homespun dress. "Do we leave behind these fine moth-eaten cloaks with the fur falling off in patches?"

"We shall have to have cloaks," decided Susanna, not heeding her sister's sarcasm. "The baby will have to have blankets too, poor little thing. Now that is all. Come quickly."

Susanna wrapped the baby warmly, and Captive,

delighted to be going anywhere, smiled up into her mother's worried face. Her happy chirruping was the only sound as they left the pretty room and made their way down the stairs into the snowy street. Once outside, Susanna's determination suddenly petered out, and she leaned weakly against the wall.

"I was in such haste to be rid of that place. Now I don't know where to turn. Where do you think we could find work, Miriam?"

"Do you think the Mayor's wife?" Miriam ventured. "She might let you take care of Polly."

The quick spark of hope in Susanna's eyes died away. "No chance of that. The woman will never let me lay eyes on my child if she can help it. No, we

have had enough of the fine folks. If we're to find work it will have to be with our own kind."

"Then we'll try the shops," Miriam decided. "There is one where I bought thread. That woman was friendly."

They were thoroughly chilled by the time they had made their way down the hill to the Rue de St. Paul, and they thankfully entered the steamy warmth of the shop. But the woman's friendly smile died away at their first words.

"Work? But certainly not. Do you think I cannot care for this little shop by myself? What could I want with two women and a baby?"

What would anyone want with two strange women and a baby? It was not only indifference they met, from shop to shop, but a definite hostility which struck as coldly to their spirits as the biting wind they had to return to time after time. When finally they stopped and huddled close to a wall for warmth, Miriam met Susanna's eyes over the bundle of blanket, and saw there a reflection of the panic that was rising in her like a sickness.

"Those soldiers!" she shuddered. "They have passed us three times now. I don't like the way they look at us."

Susanna bit her lip. "We must keep moving, or they will suspect we have nowhere to go. For all we know they may have orders to put us in jail."

It was fast growing dark. Captive, cold and ravenous, set up a piercing wail that would not be quieted. Hurrying down the alleyway, Miriam glanced behind and saw a dark figure following them. Her heart sank, and then all at once bounded with relief. It was not a soldier pursuing them but Hortense! As she came nearer her anxious round face broke into smiling wrinkles.

"Thank goodness! I thought I would never find you. For hours I have looked. Miriam, why did you go without telling me?"

"Oh, Hortense! You mean you have come all this way in the cold just to say goodbye?"

"But certainly not goodbye," said Hortense in amazement. "I have come to take you home."

"Home? Back to the Du Quesnes'?"

"To my family's house. It is not too far. Just outside the city."

Miriam felt a hot sting of tears against her eyelids. But Susanna stared at the French girl doubtfully.

"You are very kind," she said. "But we need to find work. Perhaps you know someone who would hire us?"

"Hire? You mean pay you wages?" asked Hortense incredulously. "But who would pay wages to the English?"

So the enmity in these people's faces had not been imagination!

167

"Didn't you know?" she went on, seeing their shocked faces. "Up there on the hill you did not think about the war, no? But down here, we know there is a war. You think it is safe for two English women to be wandering about on the street?"

Susanna, her face pinched with cold and despair, could not seem to make up her mind. Hortense stamped her snowy boots impatiently.

"*Allons!* We can't stand here. Give me the baby. She is a heavy one, that Captive." She started briskly down the street and they had no choice but to follow.

"But Hortense," protested Miriam, almost running to keep up, "if people feel like that — what will your family think? If we are enemies — "

"That is different," answered Hortense over her shoulder. "You are not my enemy. You are my friend, *n'est-ce pas?*"

CHAPTER 14

Beyond the city walls there was no shelter from the icy winds that roared along the black wastes of the river. Darkness closed down around them, so that the whitewashed cottages were indistinguishable from the snowy banks. Stumbling behind Hortense, Miriam and Susanna had all they could do to keep on their feet against the wind. Snow flicked up from the drifts to sting their faces. Breath was too painful to spend on any words. Then all at once, when every step had become a battle, there was firelight streaming from a welcoming door.

Black-haired children catapulted from every corner of the small room to hurl themselves at Hortense. Behind them stepped a short, sturdy woman who looked exactly as Hortense would look when her crisp hair was flecked with gray and the crinkles of her face worn deeper with years of smiling.

"This is the English friend I told you of, Maman," Hortense explained. "She and Madame Johnson have no place to go, so I have brought them home."

169

There was just the barest instant of hesitation. Then, with a cluck of sympathy, the woman reached and took the baby in her arms. *"C'est bien,"* she said. "Poor babe!"

The hearth fire was stirred to a blaze and the blood crept stingingly back into their toes and fingers. Captive blubbered noisily at a dipper of warm milk. Presently they all sat down to a feast of smoked eels, boiled potatoes, and turnips. Around the scrubbed board table Miriam learned the names of the children in order — Jean, Alphonse, Claudette, Simone, and last of all little Albert, whose cocky mischievous face must have reminded Susanna achingly of her own small son.

"You have other children?" asked Hortense's mother, noting Susanna's wistful glance. In all these months no one had ever encouraged Susanna to talk about her children, and now, under the sympathy that shone in the older woman's face, the story poured out, of Polly whom she was forbidden to see, of Sue, who was fast being wooed from her, and of Sylvanus, torn from her in the forest. There were tears in both women's eyes as she finished. Ashamed at her lack of control, Susanna rose from the table, and all at once her glance fell on the loom set up in the corner. She walked across to it, ran her hand lovingly over the worn beams, tested the taut threads, and gently lifted the shuttle.

"This reminds me of home," she said, her voice unsteady. "Would you allow me to weave a little?"

Through the days that followed Susanna sat at the loom. Hour after hour she thrust the shuttle back and forth through the strands, as though the familiar motions soothed the thoughts that tormented her. Hortense's mother, a widow struggling to be both father and mother to her brood of six, was grateful for the help. Captive, released from the confining basket, soon began to scramble about on the floor on all fours. Miriam, however, could not be reconciled. At first she waited, hour after hour, for some word from Felicité. Surely, she persuaded herself, her softhearted friend would forget her sulks, would forgive her and send for her to sit once more in the white and blue bedroom. Common sense told her that this was unreasonable, but the foolish hope died hard.

You should have known it was not for you, she railed at herself. Felicité can ride in the carriage and have a beautiful dress for every day in the week, but

171

if you ever so much as get one pretty thing 'tis snatched away from you.

Finally, envying the peace that seemed to come to Susanna at the loom, she turned in desperation to the woolen cloth. The coarse fabric gave her no pleasure. She yearned for the soft feel of satin against her fingers. But in spite of herself she began to take an interest in planning and cutting the cloth to fit the varying shapes and sizes of the boys and girls. It took ingenuity to turn and piece so that not a precious scrap would be wasted. As the days went by she made a surprising discovery. For her there was something deeply satisfying in a neat, well-finished garment, even in a tiny jumper of homespun wool. With a needle in her hand she was almost content.

Moreover, there was a warm, close friendliness and affection in the cottage that was contagious. It was impossible to follow her bitter thoughts while three admiring little girls hung over her shoulder. Instead she threaded needles for them and set them to competing for the straightest line of stitches. Gradually her hurt began to heal.

Three weeks went by. Both Miriam and Susanna knew that this interlude of snug peace could not last. Though they had been freely welcomed and made a part of the family, there were unmistakable signs that something was very wrong.

The first sign came the morning when Miriam,

crossing the snowy yard, was startled by a stinging blow on the ear. She looked down at the brown trickle that stained her cloak. That had not been a snowball! It was a handful of icy mud from a thawed patch of roadway. Across the street clustered the neighbor's children, their small faces scowling and sullen.

"You must not mind them," Hortense's mother apologized, helping to sponge the mud from the cloak. "The children don't understand that you are not to blame for the war."

On Hortense's next visit, a few days later, Miriam overheard an even more troubling remark. Coming around the corner of the house, she could not avoid hearing the last words of something that Alphonse was earnestly relating to Hortense.

" — and then they said that not one of the men would help with the plowing if they are here — "

Hortense did not like being questioned about it. "It is nothing," she explained reluctantly. "Since my father died, every spring the neighbors have plowed the land and made it ready for Maman to plant."

"And they will not do it now because we are living here?"

"They say they will not help to feed the English. Oh dear, don't worry about it. The land will be plowed. Jules will help."

Susanna had come to the end of the weaving. Every

173

inch of last year's woolen was used up, and till spring shearing there would be no more work for her to do. That was not all.

"You know," she whispered to Miriam that night, "that no matter how busy she is Madame never lets us go into the storeroom? Well, today there was such a caterwauling I ran in there without thinking. Albert, the rascal, had his finger caught under the lid of the eel barrel. I couldn't help seeing. The barrel is almost empty. It's been worrying me how all the food is divided so carefully and not one of the children ever asks for more. Miriam, there's such a pitiful little, flour or vegetables or anything. Nowhere near enough for seven mouths, let alone three extra, and the snow not even off the ground. We can't stay here and watch these good people go hungry. Tomorrow I am going to try to see the Governor himself."

An unexpected visitor, however, discouraged this plan. Peter Labaree appeared at the cottage door, looking thin and aged, the hair under his woolen cap snow-white. He had heard of their whereabouts, he told them, from a young man named Jules, whom he had met in the market.

"There's been a new Governor since we came," he said, "and I shouldn't advise going to see him. An English prisoner at the farm where I am appealed to him because he was too ill to work and was thrown in jail and kept there five weeks before they would even listen to his case. There's a powerful bad feeling against the English these days."

Miriam had an idea. It had been at the edge of her mind for some days, and she had been trying not to face it squarely.

"There is something I think perhaps I could do," she said now. "There is just one thing I need, Peter. Could you manage to get me a bit of paper and some ink?"

Peter reached into his pocket and handed her a small coin. " 'Tis a bit I won on a wager," he explained, with a guilty glance toward Susanna. "You're welcome to it, if 'twill help."

CHAPTER 15

THE FIRST gentleness of April was in the warm sunshine as Miriam hurried along the river road next morning. She had managed to get away without giving her astonished sister the slightest hint of what she intended to do. Drawing in deep breaths of the sparkling air, Miriam felt astonished at herself. It was a new thing for her to step out so independently. Somehow, in the past month a tough little root of determination had been growing in her. Whether it was strong enough to support the desperate plan she had undertaken she would soon find out. As she walked, her mind went back over every detail. Not one item must be left to chance.

Inside the city of Montreal she slowed to an inconspicuous pace. She dared not enter the shops alone, but just as she had anticipated, the streets were soon lively with customers. Waiting till a group of women, their tongues wagging, entered one of the shops, she slipped in behind them. Once inside she did her best to remain unnoticed, watching and listening, her eager mind snatching at every scrap of gossip. She even managed to finger with delight the costly materials that tumbled from half-rolled bolts on the shelves. At the first suspicious glance she slipped away, lingering in the street till another group of women gave her a similar opportunity. By the end of the morning she had learned all she needed to know. Finally she exchanged Peter Labaree's coin for a sheet of paper and a small pot of ink.

Carrying her purchases carefully, she went in search of a place to work. At last, hidden behind the half-rotted wall of an abandoned warehouse, she found a spot where she could spread the paper and balance the ink pot on a smooth weather-beaten plank.

In the early afternoon, the precious paper carefully folded in the pocket of her skirt, she set out again. Her fingers were numb with cold and she had had nothing to eat since dawn, but cold and hunger were weaknesses she could not bother with now. This time she left the Rue de St. Paul, climbed the hill past the stone houses, and lifted the great brass knocker of the Du Quesne mansion.

"Once I would have said I'd rather starve!" she muttered, but when the door opened she did not hesitate.

"I should like to speak to Madame Du Quesne," she announced, so firmly that after only a moment's indecision the footman let her in.

Miriam waited, not daring to sit on one of the gilt chairs, whose knobby curlicues her back remembered so well. If Madame refused to see her, the plan failed. But Madame rustled in, white head erect, pale blue eyes as disdainful as on the night she first confronted the hungry prisoner reeking of bear grease in her kitchen.

"I thought it was understood you would not come again to this house."

Miriam's eyes did not waver. If she allowed Madame to ruffle her, even so slightly, her plan was doomed.

"I did not expect to come," she answered pleasantly. "But I have reason to think I can be of service to you."

"You are mistaken. Our charity has already exceeded all reason."

"I am not talking of charity," Miriam answered. Under the folds of her homespun skirt her fingers ached, so tightly were they clenched down on her struggling Willard pride.

"What, then?"

"I have heard there is to be a ball when the Governor visits Montreal next fortnight. They say it is to be a very grand affair."

"It can hardly concern you."

"I should like to make gowns for you and Felicité to wear."

Madame's eyebrows raised. "We have a dress-maker," she replied. "She came to New France expressly to sew for my mother, and she has made all our gowns since I was younger than Felicité."

"She is a very fine dressmaker," Miriam acknowledged. "But she has no imagination. Your clothes and Felicité's she makes just alike, and no different from those of all the other ladies who will be there. You should have a dress that shows your height and your fine straight back to advantage. But Felicité is much shorter. Her throat and shoulders are too pretty to spoil with bunchy frills. Let me show you."

Before Madame could interrupt, Miriam drew from her pocket the folded paper with the two sketches she had made. "This is the way I would make a dress for you, with long lines here, and the panniers set just here. This one is for Felicité. There is a fresh bolt of fine muslin, just come from France, with tiny blue flowers."

Madame knit her brows over the drawings. "How do you know you could do this?" she demanded finally. "Where could you possibly have learned such skill in your English colonies?"

"I don't know how I learned," Miriam answered honestly. "But I know I can do it. I promise you that."

Madame's eyes followed the penned lines shrewdly. Miriam could see that her interest was caught.

179

Madame must know as well as Miriam that her mother's dressmaker had long since lost the Paris touch. She needed no reminder that the uncivilized English girl, with a few deft alterations, had made her appear frumpy and unfashionable. Much as she despised Miriam, she wanted these dresses. Behind that coldly expressionless mask, Miriam sensed the conflict. Spitefulness and vanity. Had she been right to gamble on the latter?

Finally Madame spoke. "This might please Felicité," she said. "Yes, I shall allow you to attempt this one dress. Only on trial, you understand. We shall see how it looks."

Miriam took a deep breath. "The dress will cost two louis," she said slowly. "And I must have half of that in advance."

Madame froze. "Two louis! Outrageous! You expect that I am to *pay* you for making this? After all we have done for you?"

Miriam forced her voice to remain pleasant. "Indeed, Madame, I am grateful for all you did for my sister and me. But now we must work for our food. You pay your dressmaker much more than that, I am certain."

"Impossible! Gamble two louis on a girl who never laid eyes on a fashionable gown before she came into my house? Why, you learned here all the fashion you know. Such impertinence!"

Miriam moved toward the door. Her whole body felt stiff. She had one more card to play, and she put her hand on the latch to steady herself.

"I am sorry that you feel I am ungrateful," she said. "It was only in fairness that I came to you first. But I must make my living with my needle. Madame the Mayor's wife was full of praises for the dresses I made over. I believe she will be glad to have me make one for her."

It was a desperate bluff. If it failed, she would never in the world have the courage to call on the Mayor's wife or anyone else. But somehow she must get away from the house before Madame guessed that. She was almost out the door when the ruse succeeded.

"*Tiens!*" said Madame. "I will do it. To please Felicité only. But you are to give me your word. Not a soul shall know that you made the dress. I would be the laughingstock of the town."

The sudden victory left Miriam's knees weak. But she must win one more point.

"I shall need one louis in advance," she said, "to buy the goods and the thread, and to pay rent on a small room."

For a moment Madame Du Quesne's indignation flared again. Then she drew a mesh bag from her skirts, took out a coin, and, with deliberate contempt, tossed it on the floor at Miriam's feet. Miriam's face went white. The Willard pride almost escaped her taut grip. Then she stooped and picked up the coin.

Outside, on the street, she could scarcely make her way for the smarting tears that blinded her. The two louis that Madame begrudged were nothing to what this victory had cost her English prisoner!

She had one more stop to make. That morning she had noticed a sign at the door of a dingy tailor's shop, CHAMBRE A LOUER. She located the shop now and knocked boldly on the door. Reluctantly the tailor showed her the room. It was small and dismal, furnished with a wooden bedstead, a rickety chair, and a crude bench. There was a window high in the wall,

letting in enough light so that she would not need to burn a candle by day. The place was dirty, but a good scrubbing would remedy that. Miriam's businesslike manner and the good hard coin in her hand overcame the tailor's suspicions.

"We shall be here tomorrow morning," she assured him.

She was thankful for the long walk home in spite of her empty stomach. By the time she reached the cottage her heart had stopped pounding, her breath was coming evenly, and she was able to announce to Susanna, quite nonchalantly, "You need not worry about the jail for a while at least. You and I are going to be dressmakers. The most fashionable dressmakers in Montreal."

CHAPTER 16

"I𝘁 IS ALL very well for you," said Susanna, ducking her head to bite the thread. "But if I sew seams for the rest of my life I shall never be a dressmaker. I can't take a stitch without this plaguey thread knotting up."

Imperceptibly, in the fortnight they had spent in this little room, their relationship had changed. It was Miriam, the "little sister," who crossed the room now to inspect the length of goods in Susanna's lap and to speak with unconscious authority.

"If you would only try to like it you wouldn't always have to do the dullest parts. These rosettes are just play, really. Try one, Susanna."

"Not I. I'll stick to the plain seams and the mending the tailor parcels out to us, and leave the fancy trimmings to you."

Miriam expertly twisted the blue satin into another of the tiny flowers that dotted the ruffled skirt. "I hope it will be fair tomorrow," she said. " 'Twill be a pity to cover this lovely thing with a woolen cloak. What is May Day about, anyway, Susanna?"

" 'Tis a heathen custom," said Susanna. "Though I've heard tell they celebrate it in England too. Scandalous, some of the things that go on. Though I must say, I can't see much harm in a little dancing around a Maypole. If I had my girls now, I'd be minded to let them do that much."

"I'm going with Hortense tomorrow," said Miriam hurriedly, to forestall the tears that always sprang so quickly to Susanna's eyes at every thought of her children. "Why don't you come too, Susanna? 'Twould do you good to have a holiday and to get Captive out in the fresh air. We could work a little later tonight, maybe."

Susanna did not answer. It was getting harder every day to think of ways to rouse Susanna from the despair that held her like a net, drawing ever tighter. At first the springtime had brought her a brief hope. The ice cracked and drifted on the great river, and the breezes that found their way through the high window of the room were sweet with promise. But now they knew that Indian canoes crossed the river freely every day. There was no longer any excuse for the long silence.

"Look," Miriam coaxed now, holding the dress up against her. "Isn't it pretty, Susanna? Even prettier than I imagined."

185

Susanna's eyes held a flicker of surprise, not at the dress but at her sister's eager face.

"You sound as though you enjoy it," she accused. "When I look at it, all I can think of is the six times you ripped out those gathers, and the extra candles we had to burn because you had to have it just so."

"I won't have to another time," said Miriam. "I've learned how it's done now. 'Tis a queer thing, but I do enjoy it, almost. When I started this dress I hated every inch of it because it was for Felicité and I could never wear it myself. But now 'tis done I'm rather fond of it."

"You see," she went on, wanting to share with her sister a thought that was only beginning to be clear in her own mind, "I feel as though I own it, even though I can't ever see it again. I made it up out of nothing. In a way it is mine more than it is Felicité's. I suppose you'll say that's pride."

"Yes," said Susanna, " 'tis pride, I suppose. But I don't know but some kinds of pride are good and natural. I used to feel that way when we planted the garden. And when we built the cabin, where there'd been only trees and underbrush before. The best cabin at Number Four, everyone said."

And down went Susanna's head into her hands. Miriam felt at once impatient and ashamed. How could she expect Susanna to take any pleasure in a

186

dress that only meant food enough to eke out this miserable waiting? Nearly six months, and no word from James. Though the fear could never be put into words, Miriam knew that her sister believed her husband dead. Susanna had shared the long hours of work, the bitter cold that stiffened their fingers at daybreak, the smoky candlelight that tortured their eyes at night, but she could never share the unreasonable pride of creation that was Miriam's recompense.

"I'll deliver the dress now," said Miriam, folding it carefully inside a worn length of bedding. "I might as well get it over with. This is the part I hate most. If Madame pays me at all she will manage to make me feel like a worm. Try to sleep a little while I'm gone, Susanna."

Her brief mood of satisfaction evaporated as she climbed the hill. Could she coax another order from Madame today? The gay winter season of parties was over. Ships from France were soon due, and the shops would be replenished with the latest finery. Luck was with her, however. Though Madame refused to see her, she sent a message by way of the footman.

"Madame says you may come on Friday to begin the fittings for her gown," he reported.

Praise be, Madame had remembered to leave the louis d'or.

As she turned away from the door into the street,

a chance encounter swept away the last particle of satisfaction. A smart little carriage was drawing up to the doorway. It passed so close that as she flattened herself against the wall the muddy wheels just grazed her skirt, and the three occupants could scarcely help but see her. Madame Du Quesne stared straight ahead with no sign of recognition. Felicité, the ribbon bows of the first straw hat of the season tied under her pretty chin, parted her red lips in an involuntary greeting that suddenly froze in remembrance. She turned deliberately to the man beside her. It was Pierre Laroche, his dark, lively gaze intent on Felicité's lifted face. Miriam bent her head. The moment the wheel cleared her path she turned and sped down the hill. Had he recognized her? From the day she had returned to Montreal she had dreaded such a meeting. But with just a moment's warning she could surely have managed better. Right now he and Felicité must be laughing with merriment at the way she had scuttled down the street. The thought slowed her to a decent gait.

With an effort she forced her mind back to the arithmetic that occupied so much of her thoughts of late. Rent to the tailor, brown bread at twenty sols a loaf, milk for Captive, vegetables that would be scarce and costly till the new crop was grown. How far would one coin stretch? Would there be enough for the shoes Susanna must have, or for calico to make a thin dress for each of them for the hot months ahead? She would stop and look at the bolts of goods, at least, though she dared not purchase any.

Lingering in the shops was her one indulgence, and she had wasted more than an hour when finally she returned to the room. She felt a twinge of remorse at finding Susanna still hard at work. Unwrapping the bread, she stooped to put a hard bun into the baby's hand, and Captive displayed her two new teeth in an enchanting smile. She would put the meeting with Felicité entirely out of her mind, Miriam decided; it was not even worth mentioning to her sister.

Suddenly there were rushing footsteps and agitated voices in the shop, and without a knock their door was flung open. For a moment neither of them could recognize the distracted woman who confronted them. It was the Mayor's wife, her coiffure awry, a cloak clutched at her throat.

"Give me back my child!" she demanded.

The heavy coat Susanna was mending slid to the floor with a thud.

"I know she is here!" the woman cried. "It is no good for you to hide her."

Miriam found her voice. "Polly? Are you talking about Polly?"

"Alphonsine! My coachman saw you going down

the street. She must have followed you."

"But I did not see her at all. Are you sure she is gone?"

Susanna had not spoken a word. The woman stared from one to the other. Even in her frantic state she was forced to believe their bewilderment. Suddenly, with a frightened gasp, she sank against the wall.

"Then where can she be? I was sure that if we tracked you down — and now all this time wasted!"

"Polly ran away?" Susanna managed to speak at last.

"She has run away twice before, but we have soon found her. She is so little, and she has never been about in the town. She dashes so fast, I am afraid of the horses. She could be crushed under their feet."

Susanna was pulling on her shoes. "We will find her," she said. "Get a blanket for the baby, Miriam. I daren't leave her alone."

Out on the street a carriage was waiting. "My coachman has gone to every house on the hill," the Mayor's wife explained. "I have sent a servant out along the road to the west. I will take the carriage and drive out the east road." The whip cracked over the horse's head.

For a moment Miriam and Susanna faced each other helplessly. They were more familiar with the streets now. They knew that Montreal was not the vast city it had seemed. But there were a thousand corners where a small child could be hidden.

"I'll go this way," Susanna decided. "Ask everyone you meet."

Miriam hurried along the Rue de St. Paul, stopping to question citizens she would never have dreamed of addressing. Back along the devious route she had come, into the dress shops where she had visited, down the alleyways that led away from the main thoroughfare she searched. The business of the day was drawing to a close. Shopkeepers were pulling the curtains and locking their doors. No, no one had seen a child. Gradually the streets began to clear of people hurrying home to their suppers. Miriam and Susanna met again, and separated once more. She would try the warehouse section this time.

The sun was quite low behind the warehouses when Miriam had the first encouraging sign. "Yes, we saw a child this afternoon," a cluster of children admitted, pointing vaguely in the direction of the river. "She went that way. She had on a white dress."

Hope flaring, Miriam followed the path that led to the landing beach, peering with a shudder into the dark doorways of the storehouses, till she came out on the strip of beach and the shimmering river. The beach was deserted. Some distance away four fishermen were dragging in their boat. Their quick shouts and the rasp of the keel against the pebbles was loud in the evening air. In the opposite direction stretched a line of crude sheds, and toward them Miriam turned, her heart sinking.

Then her glance went back to the beach and held. Drawn up close to the water were two Indian canoes, and in one of them she caught a flash of white. She broke into a run across the hard sand, and stumbled with a cry of thanksgiving against the canoe. Curled up on a soft pile of skins Polly lay sound asleep, her red curls shining against the black fur.

Polly felt very light as Miriam lifted her in her arms, almost as light as the baby Captive. After one startled stiffening of her small body, her arms wrapped suffocatingly about Miriam's neck. It was impossible to persuade her to walk, so the way from the beach was slow. It was growing dark when they neared the tailor shop, and Miriam saw that the carriage had returned. Madame and Susanna stood close together on the pavement, their enmity forgotten. At sight of Miriam both women sprang forward. But Miriam, without the slightest hesitation, unwrapped Polly's clinging arms and gave her into Susanna's yearning grasp. Susanna sank down on the doorstep, unable to make a single sound, rocking back and forth, her dark head bent over the shining curls.

Madame the Mayor's wife stood looking down at

them, her face distorted with pain. Then suddenly she turned away.

"I never knew," she choked. "To lose a child — it is unbearable! But I thought she would forget and come to love me instead."

Miriam felt unexpected pity. "Most children would have, I think," she said gently. "I know you have been good to her."

"I will send her clothes tomorrow," the woman said.

Without thinking, Miriam put her hand on the woman's arm. "You mean you are going to let us keep Polly? Oh madame — !"

"Let us not talk about it!" the Mayor's wife flung at her. As she climbed into the carriage, tears were streaming down her cheeks.

That night Susanna bent to hold the candle close to the faces of her sleeping children, as though she could not believe without looking again and again that there were two of them where only Captive had slept before.

"I believe that God has sent her back to me as a reminder," she said humbly. "I am ashamed that I have despaired in my heart. I shall never doubt His goodness again."

CHAPTER 17

Mᴀʏ Dᴀʏ could not lure Susanna away from the tailor shop. " 'Tis all the celebration I want just to look at my two little ones," she insisted. "I have no desire to go traipsing about the streets. Go along, Miriam, and have a good time with Hortense."

For once Miriam could leave her sister with a lighter heart. Even the unholiday drabness of the homespun dress could not dim the expectation with which she set out soon after daybreak.

Hortense, in her Sunday calico skirt, was waiting at the city gates. Her feet sped even more impatiently than Miriam's, and presently the sturdy figure of Jules came hastening along the road to meet them. How fine Jules looked in a tall beaver hat that added both inches and dignity! He greeted them courteously, but his eyes were only on Hortense.

"You are just in time," he warned. "They are about to raise the Maypole."

In front of a substantial whitewashed house, the largest and best in the parish, habitants from cottages along the road were gathered, farmers and their wives, young folk, and countless darting, bright-cheeked children. Two perspiring young men were just flinging the last shovels of dirt from a yawning hole in the ground before the house. A noisy throng of boys and young men and a few hardy girls came dragging a tall fir tree, all its branches stripped away to the top, which still flaunted a tuft of green. It required much heaving and shoving, and much shouting of encouragement and advice, to lift the tree and set it in place and heap the dirt firmly about its base. Then the young men, still puffing, popped their good beaver hats on their heads, collected their muskets, and lined up for a thundering volley of shots in honor of the white-haired seigneur who watched from the doorway. This was the signal for festivities to begin. Shouting and singing, the men abandoned their muskets to swing their partners about the Maypole. Miriam, watching at the fringe, was presently swept into the thick of the dancing, as partners changed so briskly from hand to hand that friends and strangers were caught up. How good it was to dance again! Not the mincing steps of the minuet that Felicité had taught her, but the lively, heel-tapping, hand-clapping measures that had shaken the rafters that night at Number Four. They set her blood racing, the chestnut curls flying out behind her, and the homespun dress twirling as gaily as any holiday dress in the parish.

196

"Would you like to come with us, Miriam?" Hortense invited as the merrymakers began to drift away toward their own homes. "Even though it is a holiday we must work. Jules is going to help mother and me to do our planting. Mother would be so glad to see you."

Miriam hesitated. The dancing had stirred in her the restlessness she had sternly subdued for the past weeks. She chafed at the prospect of spending her holiday tagging along, a third person, on the rare day that Hortense and Jules could spend together.

"I promised Susanna I wouldn't be away long," she fibbed. "Besides, I have a new order from Madame to start on."

"You are so smart, Miriam," Hortense admired.

"But you will come to our wedding? Promise you will! The second Saturday in June it will be. Jules has the house all ready."

Smiling at the pride and happiness that shone in her friend's face, Miriam promised. They were not really sorry to see her go. They stood hand in hand and gaily waved her goodbye.

Inside the city the holiday spirit had taken over. Shops were closed for the day, shopkeepers and their wives and children, furriers, hatmakers, bakers, and tinsmiths, picnic baskets on their arms, were headed for the country. From one side of the street to the other greetings and laughter were exchanged. No one on this spring morning seemed to be alone. The promise that had filled the air at daybreak seemed to be fulfilled for everyone but her. Moreover, Miriam noticed uneasily that the streets were swarming with Indians, more than she had ever seen before in Montreal. They carried moccasins and baskets and embroidered belts, even pelts of animals, to trade with any passer-by who stopped to look. Apparently French brandy was as welcome a currency as coin, for already many of the Indians were swaggering unsteadily. Better for her to spend the day with Susanna in the safety of the small room.

A figure planted itself suddenly and directly in her path, a tall figure in a white uniform with scarlet facings. There was nothing Miriam could do but look up to face the one pair of bold black eyes she most dreaded to meet.

"So it is you!" Pierre Laroche triumphed. "I thought so yesterday, but Felicité she said no. Where have you hidden yourself all this time?"

"I have not been hiding," she answered in confusion.

Not well enough, anyway. Now the damage was done, and those deliberate eyes of his were not missing a single detail of the dingy homespun, the much mended kerchief, the pricked and calloused fingers.

"I always suspected they had turned you out," he said finally. "Felicité said you had been ransomed and gone back to the English."

"I expect we will be," she said airily. "Any day now."

His glance took that for what it was worth. "You are alone?" he inquired. "Nobody walks alone on May Day."

"My sister is waiting," Miriam answered.

"Let her wait a little. The dancing has given me a thirst. Stop in here and have a drink of wine with me at least. You owe me that for the time I have spent looking for you."

Miriam shook her head in panic.

"But what am I thinking of? You are a Puritan, *n'est-ce pas?* Some chocolate, then?"

199

She was ashamed even to hesitate. But the door of the nearby grogshop was open, and from it drifted a sweetish steaming fragrance that made her head swim. In that second of hesitation he had seized her elbow.

"A cup of chocolate," he ordered, of the woman who tended the copper kettle.

Oh, that luscious, rich brown warmth! Miriam forced herself to sip daintily, but his bright eyes were knowing.

"It becomes you to be thin," he said, "but you need not fade away altogether. A second cup for mademoiselle," he added, tossing a coin on the counter.

"*Alors,*" he said, as she drained the last sweet drop. "You have never seen anything like this in your colonies, have you? Let me show you about a little."

Miriam hung back. "I should be working," she told him. "Besides, there are too many Indians to suit me."

Pierre laughed. "Are you afraid with an officer of the King beside you? Just a few moments! It is not May Day every day."

In spite of herself a smile broke through Miriam's shyness. Her high spirits were not so far below the surface, after all; they were certainly not proof against such urging.

"*Bien,* that is better," he approved, and as they stepped into the street he tucked her hand expertly into his elbow.

The noisy street had lost its menacing aspect. From the protection of Pierre's uniformed elbow Miriam began to enjoy the spectacle. Pierre moved along the pavement, greeting citizen and Indian alike with a cocky familiarity.

"You actually know these Indians!" Miriam exclaimed.

"Why are you so skittish about the Indians, anyway? Did they treat you so badly?"

"No, they didn't," Miriam admitted. "It was entirely different from what we expected. But you can't trust them. You never know what they'll do the next minute."

"That shows you don't understand them. You have to learn to get along with the Indians. That's something you English have never bothered to try."

"But why should we?" Miriam countered, astonished at the idea. Pierre shrugged.

"That depends. It is the Indians' country, *n'est-ce pas?* I know, I've watched your English traders. They go clomping through the forest in their English boots. They are bound to show the Indians who is master, even if they get scalped doing it. We French now, we have a different idea. A sort of give and take, you might call it."

"You mean you lower yourselves to their ways?"

"There you go! What makes you so sure their ways

are lower? The Indians lived in these woods long before we ever came here. They can teach us plenty. How far do you think the *coureurs* would have gone — almost as far as the great western sea — without the Indians' help?"

Pierre's free arm swept in a wide arc toward the west. "I've got Indian friends out there better than any white man I know. Don't let this uniform fool you, my girl. If I had my way I'd trade it for Indian breeches as fast as I could snap a finger."

This was strange talk for a white man! But this man was unlike anyone she had ever known before — except Mehkoa! No, she was not fooled by his uniform, nor by his manner of a nobleman. Behind them Miriam could sense the same barely tamed savagery that had never let her relax when Mehkoa was near. Pierre was as unpredictable as an Indian.

A noisy straggle of Indian boys came darting through the crowd in a boisterous game of tag. Miriam drew instinctively nearer her companion to avoid them, but as they passed, she caught an unmistakable flash of bright blue eyes.

"Sylvanus!" she screamed, recognition quicker than thought.

Involuntarily the boy checked at the name and turned to glare at her. Was she right? The eyes in his brown, dirt-streaked face were brilliant blue, but there was not a sign of recognition in them.

"Sylvanus! 'Tis Miriam! Don't you know me?" He whipped round suddenly and dashed after his companions.

"Pierre!" she cried, in her urgency gripping the white uniformed sleeve. "Get him for me — oh please!"

Pierre did not stop to question. He was after the boy in a bound, with Miriam racing and twisting close behind. Except for a group of soldiers who checked the racing boys, they would soon have lost the race. Hemmed in, the boys stopped to get their bearings, and as Miriam caught up, Pierre faced her with a kicking, clawing little savage held firmly by the neck of his deerskin jacket.

"Hold still, you little weasel!" he ordered. "The lady wants to look at you."

She was not mistaken. That stub nose and square little chin had to belong to Sylvanus. Under the stained matted hair Miriam could see the new blond growth close to the scalp.

"Sylvanus!" she coaxed. "Come with me. I'll take you to Mother!"

In answer Sylvanus ducked his head, sank his teeth into the hand that gripped him, and in one twisting brown arc was gone.

"The little devil!" Pierre cursed, sucking the blood from his hand. Miriam leaped into pursuit, but in a few steps she had lost every trace. Not an Indian boy was in sight. Her scorn blazed out.

"You let him go on purpose! Don't tell me a great soldier like you — and a *coureur* at that — couldn't get the better of one little boy!"

Pierre shrugged. "I've no liking to see any animal in captivity," he said deliberately.

"But he *is* in captivity! He's an English boy! He's my nephew!" She was sobbing hysterically. Pierre laid a hand on her shoulder.

"Did he look like a captive? He is free as the air, like a young fox cub. Think a moment, Miriam. What were you going to do with him? Pen him up in some hole with a couple of women? Do you want to turn him into skin and bones like you?"

"I don't understand you!" Miriam sobbed. "He is a white boy. He belongs to us, to his own people, and he's growing up to be a savage!"

"What if he is?" demanded Pierre. "You and your talk about savages! He's living the best life a boy could have, and I would to heaven I could change places with him!"

Miriam raised a shocked face. "How can you talk so?" she gasped. "Are you a Christian?"

"You disappoint me," he returned coldly. "The first time I saw you you reminded me of an Indian girl. 'There is one who is not like the others,' I said to myself. But now you talk like all the rest."

"There is no reason for our talking any more then," Miriam said. "Let me go now. I can find my way back by myself."

But Pierre walked beside her, guiding her through the crowd, and would not be shaken until they reached the door of the tailor shop.

"So this is where you live," he said. "I wanted to know because I am coming again. One thing more. If you are the sensible girl I take you for, you will say nothing to the boy's mother. I know Indians; he is already so well hidden that she would never find a hair of him, never."

Miriam turned to face him with scorn. "Don't bother to come again," she said icily. "If you do, I shall refuse to see you."

There was merriment in Pierre's eyes. Plainly he could not credit such a statement from any girl.

"You say that now because you are angry with me," he conceded. "But you and I, we are more alike than you think. You will see me again."

He was off down the street, the arrogant swing of the *coureur* unhampered by the officer's uniform.

With her hand on the latch Miriam paused. How could she hide from Susanna all that had happened? How could her sister fail to sense the excitement that shouted in the air around her like clanging bells?

Could she give an account of the Maypole dance that would explain the blood that pounded in her cheeks and the hand that refused to hold steady? One hint about Sylvanus and there would be no holding her sister. Susanna would search the streets until she dropped exhausted, and Miriam knew in that much at least Pierre had spoken truly. She would never find a trace of him.

Susanna, however, was too preoccupied to spare more than a hasty greeting as she entered. She was spooning a sticky gruel into Captive's unwilling mouth, painstakingly scraping up every drop that dribbled off the small chin.

"There is only enough for one," she said.

Miriam noticed how the two lines cutting deeper between Susanna's eyebrows gave her an irritable look so unfair to her generous nature.

"The baby will have to get this gruel down, like it or not. Polly has been whining for chocolate all the morning. 'Tis no use explaining that we can't get it. She doesn't understand a word I say. I truly wonder, Miriam, did we do right? She needs all the good food she can get."

"Nonsense. I think she is gaining already," lied Miriam, covering up a sick plunge of guilt at the thought of the two cups of chocolate. But one question was answered. She could not tell Susanna about

Sylvanus. What could they do with him here if by some miracle they should find him? The appetite a little savage like that must have! She was as heartless as Pierre, Miriam thought, struggling to shake off his influence. But common sense added that nothing short of chains and bars could have kept Sylvanus in this airless room.

That night, lying awake beside Susanna, Miriam tried to calm her troubled conscience with the question that had never failed, through so many sleepless nights of indecision, to steady and guide her. What would Phineas Whitney say, if only she could ask him? But tonight, for the first time, the thought brought her no comfort. Even his image failed her. So many times his face had come clearly before her mind. Now, try as she would, she could not see him, or even recall the sound of his voice. Instead, against her will, another face intruded, bold, dark-eyed, disturbing. It was not the officer of the King who strode through her dreams; it was the young *coureur de bois* as she had first seen him, singing, his head thrown back, white teeth flashing.

CHAPTER 18

THE FIRST DAY of June, James Johnson returned. Without a word of warning, abruptly, his gaunt figure appeared in the doorway. For a moment they stared, not recognizing, until with a shriek Susanna sprang forward and was gathered into his arms.

Such joy was too painful to witness. But when Miriam tried to slip past them, they remembered her. Susanna snatched at the shreds of her composure, and James laid a hand on the girl's shoulder.

"Nay, do not go, sister. We have much to say, and it concerns you as well. I must hear what has happened to you both. How do you come to be in such a place?"

So, while Susanna clung unashamedly to her husband's hand, they put together the story of the past seven months. As they talked, little Captive drew herself up on the strange man's knee, and when he lifted her gently, gazed with her irresistible trusting smile into his bearded face. But Polly clung wailing to her mother and refused to let him touch her.

"Little Susanna?" questioned James.

"She is still with the two sisters. Oh, James, she is a little French child, and I fear she has forgotten us altogether. But now that you have come we shall get her back again."

He had been in Boston all winter, James explained. After leaving Montreal in November he had gone directly to Albany and then on to Boston to apply to Governor Shirley for money to redeem his family. He had waited through an intolerable delay while the matter was laid before the General Assembly, and had finally been granted one hundred and fifty pounds and given a letter of credit and a passport. He had proceeded halfway across Massachusetts when an order from Governor Shirley caught up with him. Because the war had commenced in earnest it was unsafe to go on, and he must return to Boston at once. There, in spite of repeated appeals, he had been forced to stay all winter and spring. Finally he had made such a nuisance of himself that he had been permitted, against all advice, to set out for Canada. Most of the journey he had made alone and on foot.

Then in turn James listened while they poured out to him the story of their own changing fortunes. The shocking treatment they had received did not surprise him.

"I am thankful you have not been actually mistreated," he said. "Conditions are far more serious

209

than you realize. England and France are beyond all hope of being reconciled. There will shortly be a fight to the finish, and we shall be caught in the thick of it if we do not leave here at once."

Susanna laid her head on his shoulder. "We must find Sylvanus," she said. "But I know we shall have him again. First Polly and now you. I shall never be afraid any more."

Suddenly Miriam felt that she could not bear to look for another moment at the naked happiness in her sister's face. "I must get bread," she said, too abruptly.

"Wait a moment," said James, reaching inside his pocket. "I have something for you. I promise you I have guarded it as close as my passport, but it has seen hard travel. I trust it can still be read, if one cares to try."

A letter for her! Miriam stared at the packet in her hand, with the thin lines of her name rubbed almost invisible. She did not know the handwriting; it was some inner perception, or perhaps only the kindly twinkle in James's eye, that brought the blood suddenly into her cheeks.

"Take it along with you and read it," said Susanna, with her old understanding. "I cannot hold another drop of news in my head just now."

Outside, in the patch of garden behind the tailor shop, Miriam summoned courage to break the seal.

Her eyes flew first to the bottom of the second page, to the name that was signed there, and for a long moment she could not read anything else. Phineas Whitney! She had never before seen with her eyes the name that had been written in her heart for so long. What a fine hand he had, delicate, yet so firm and scholarly! She drew a long breath and began the letter.

My dear Miriam:

By great good fortune I was sent with a detachment to Albany and here ran across your brother, Captain Johnson, who is to set out for Montreal in the morning. That after all these months of silence I have the opportunity to write some words which in a short time may actually rest in your hands seems a miracle. How can I choose the few words this page can contain of all the thousands that crowd my mind?

To know, after this dread waiting, that you are alive and safe is a blessing I can scarcely credit. These men tell so many pitiful stories of parents and wives and children carried off by the Indians that often it seemed vain to hope that you could have survived. I have been buoyed up by rumors of prisoners sold to the French in Montreal, and by the thought that surely your lot among Christian men and women could not have been so wretched as that of a captive in an Indian camp.

211

The very day that you and your sister's family were so cruelly set upon, I enlisted in a company of militia under Major Bellows. I had never before felt any hatred toward our Indian enemies, and truthfully, I had shrunk from the thought of warfare and killing. Now I realized that it was beyond question for me to bury myself in a world of books while such outrages were taking place in our country. Indeed, so desperate was my feeling that college would have been unendurable.

We have covered much of the country between here and Crown Point. The rigors of these forest journeys you know too well. I wondered often how you and your unfortunate sister could have endured. However, the thought that you had passed over the same hard trails, and that some deserted campfire might have been the very one that served to warm you, has comforted me through many long night watches.

I fear there are months of fighting ahead. I have not abandoned my plans for Harvard, and am determined more than ever that I shall enter the ministry, but these plans must wait. That times of quiet and decency are ahead I do not doubt, and I keep the thought ever in mind. I trust that you too, in exile, share these hopes and that you do not lose courage.

Improper as it may be in a letter which may fall

212

into other hands than yours, I cannot forbear to write something of what fills my heart. We were robbed of the little time we might have had together. I have no word of yours to assure me that our brief friendship held for you the same significance it held for me, but I must go on believing so. Every hope of the future is meaningless unless I have faith that you and I will share it together.

Whatever may lie between this day and our next meeting, I am

Faithfully yours,
PHINEAS WHITNEY

Miriam read the letter through three times. Her mind was drowning in such confusion as she had never before experienced.

In this thin packet in her hand was fulfilled every dream that she had cherished through anxious nights and weary days. Those dreams had not been illusions after all. The steadfastness, the understanding, the unspoken promise were all realities.

Why then did this letter, which a few months before would have lifted her to the clouds, now plunge her into this torment of uncertainty? Phineas had not changed. Ah, but she herself had changed! To the girl who had said goodbye at the cabin door that night so long ago, the whole world had been bounded by a new calico dress and the promise in a boy's blue eyes.

But that small world had been shattered by sights and sounds beyond anything she could have imagined. Was it possible for her ever again to be the girl that Phineas Whitney remembered? Frightening as it was, she faced the real question. Did she really want to be that girl again?

After a long time she went back to the room, without the bread she had gone to buy.

"It does not matter," whispered Susanna, a finger on her lips. "He could not stay awake even to eat." Indeed, the spare figure sprawled across the bed looked as though nothing could disturb his heavy slumber.

"He has hardly stopped to rest for days. Let him sleep now. Tomorrow will be time enough to see the Governor."

But the Governor did not wait for tomorrow. That evening at sundown three French soldiers appeared at the door, with warrants for arrest not only for James Johnson, but for Susanna his wife and their two children.

"But we are free citizens!" protested Susanna. "My husband has the letter for our release."

The men shrugged their shoulders. They had orders from the Marquis De Vaudreuil, Governor of Canada.

"Vaudreuil?" questioned James. "He is not the man I dealt with last autumn."

"He is the new Governor," a soldier volunteered.

"Then that explains the misunderstanding," said James. "Let us go peaceably, Susanna. One night in jail will not hurt us after all we have been through. In the morning everything will be straightened out."

Miriam watched the bewildered group move ahead of the soldiers: James, his step uncertain with fatigue, carrying the baby Captive, Susanna, trying to hide her terror from Polly, who dragged at her hand.

"There is no warrant for you," the soldier objected, as she prepared to follow. "The paper says you are a seamstress, employed by Monsieur Jacques, the tailor."

Numbed at the lightning turn of events, she watched from the doorway of the shop, until they were out of sight behind their guards.

By midmorning there had been no news of them, and she dared not leave the place for fear of missing some message. Repeatedly she went to the door and strained her eyes for sight of them in the narrow street. By afternoon she went in search.

Everywhere she was rebuffed. She was turned away from the jail entrance. She could not see the Mayor. When she summoned all her courage and broached the gate of the Governor's residence, the guards refused even to listen. For five days Miriam tried vainly to get some explanation. On the sixth day she realized that she must go on with her work. She had slept very little; she was desperately hungry, and should her family return there would be little to feed them. She carried an unfinished gown to Madame Du Quesne, and while she measured and pinned, she humbled herself to ask Madame's help. Madame denied having heard of James's return or of the family's whereabouts. Furthermore, she made it very clear that any concern outside of dressmaking was not to be expected from her.

Returning home that night, Miriam admitted that she could no longer let her pride keep her from turning to the one person who might be able to help her. Somehow she must reach Pierre Laroche, who was an officer in the regiment and knew everybody worth knowing in Montreal.

It took some time to compose a short note asking him to come. Then she parted with two precious copper coins to bribe a boy who hung about the shop. Certainly, yes, everybody knew the tall officer who used to be a *coureur*. He could not fail to find him. But watching the boy's meandering course down the street, Miriam had little confidence that the letter would ever reach Pierre. If he did not come, she would have to forget pride and respectability altogether and go in search of him.

CHAPTER 19

O<small>N THE THIRD EVENING</small> after she had
sent him the letter Pierre Laroche appeared jauntily
at the tailor shop.

"This is no place to talk," he decided, eying the
uncomfortable furnishings. "There is a tavern a few
doors down, where we can get more of the chocolate
you do not seem to dislike."

This time Miriam did not hesitate. She needed both
the chocolate and Pierre's good will. She was sure it
must be improper for a girl to enter the murky little
shop, but to her surprise, she found it scrubbed and
respectable. Across the small table she endured the
smug air of masculine triumph with which Pierre
appraised her. She knew exactly what he was going
to say, and he did not spare her.

"So you changed your mind about seeing me?"

"I had good reason," she answered, assuming as
businesslike a manner as she could manage.

"If I had known the letter was from you I'd have
come sooner," he went on. "When the boy brought
it there was no one about to read it for me, so I stuffed

it into my pocket and forgot all about it till I found it there tonight."

Astonishment distracted her from her purpose. "You mean — you can't read?"

Pierre bristled. "What do you take me for, a monk who spends his life with his head in a book? I told you, when I was ten years old my grandfather took me out of school to go into the trade. I can read well enough to tally up my year's accounts, never fear."

"Well, I am grateful to you for coming," Miriam hastened on, embarrassed at her rudeness. "I wrote to you because I didn't know where to turn. You see, Captain Johnson came back finally, just as I told you he would. But without even letting him explain, they took him off to prison, and Susanna and the children with him."

Pierre raised an eyebrow. "What kind of reception did your English captain think to get in Montreal?"

"But he had a letter of credit for the Governor. And a passport. He intended to take us away at once."

"How did he expect to get you back? Don't you know that the Indians on your side of the river are hungry for English scalps?"

"He had Indian guides hired to see us back."

Pierre shook his head. "Take my advice. Montreal may not just suit your fancy, but it's better than being roasted alive."

Miriam shuddered. It had not occurred to her that

219

they might not be able to reach Number Four.

"You didn't seem to find Montreal so distasteful last winter," he said. "The trouble is, a girl like you needs excitement. I wager those tailor's dummies haven't been lively enough company for you."

He had succeeded at last in bringing a reluctant smile. "That's better. What you need is to forget your troubles and step out a little. What do you say to a little party this evening? A few friends of mine —"

"In this dress?"

Pierre stared at her, confused. "You mean that is the only one you own? *Parbleu!* I'll buy you a dress!"

She stiffened instantly.

"Good heavens, girl, what's a dress? Five dresses for that matter. I guarantee, if I ask them, I can get one of the shops to open up just for you."

Miriam tightened her lips stubbornly.

"What a stuffy little Puritan you are, anyway," he flung at her. "Here I find you, after all this time, living like a stray cat, and all you do is arch your back and glare at me."

The picture of herself was too apt, and she had to laugh. Truce declared, she came seriously to the point.

"There is something you can do," she said soberly. "If you really want to help me. No one will listen. Can you get me into the jail to visit my sister?"

Pierre stared at her. Then suddenly he threw back

his head and laughed so loudly that a passing Frenchman paused in the street and peered in through the
doorway.

"What a girl!" he exclaimed. "Offer her a dress,
invite her to a party, and what does she want instead
— to go to jail."

"I'm serious, Pierre. Can you do it, please?"

"Look here, little one," he said, taking a serious tone
himself, "as far as getting your family out of that jail,
I can do nothing at all. But if you really want to go in
there and visit them, I think I can arrange that. Tomorrow morning."

Contrary to her expectations, he kept his word.
Though it was almost midday, and she had given up
hope, he came for her and conducted her along the
streets to the jail. There he spoke to the sentry, and
passed something into the man's hand.

"And mind you," Pierre repeated to the sentry, "she
comes back. In a quarter-hour. I shall be waiting
here to see that she does." That mocking glance of his
could be steely enough when he chose. With a backward glance of gratitude, Miriam stepped through the
stone gateway.

In the narrow passageway, her senses shriveled.
With every step away from the hot summer street, the
chill damp increased, until she was shivering. As they
entered the common jail, the stench struck her in the

221

face like a smothering blanket. In the half-dark she could make out huddled forms crowded close together like grotesque shadows. Their terrifying faces turned toward her, grayish white with coal-black greedy eyes. In a cell-like chamber, separated from the rest, Susanna and her husband and children sat on rough wooden benches.

They were more fearful than pleased to see her. "Are you sure you can get back out?" Susanna kept insisting. Miriam reassured her, intensely grateful, all at once, for that confident figure waiting outside.

"I will keep on trying to see everyone I can think of," she told them. "The city seems to be full of soldiers, and everyone is too busy to listen."

"I came back at the worst possible time," said James. "I am sure they are preparing for a major battle. Also, the Governor has been replaced. This new man, Monsieur De Vaudreuil, claims to know nothing whatever about the agreement. The letter of credit is absolutely worthless, so they say. Hard money they would listen to, I think. Miriam, I can pay the jailer to get me paper. I will write a letter to the Governor at Albany. Take it with you, and if you can possibly find a chance to send it —"

While James scratched at his letter in the dim light, Miriam stared about the place. The children sucked hungrily on the lumps of maple sugar she had brought in her pocket. With growing horror, Miriam saw the little stream of water dripping down the moldy wall into a dirty pool on the floor, the mats of straw covered with filthy scraps of blanket, the chipped dishes, the pail greasy with traces of soup. Her muscles quivered as a shadow moved in the corner and disappeared.

"Yes, 'tis a rat," said Susanna calmly. "But it will not come near while we are awake. James and I take turns watching at night. Captive does not know enough to be afraid, but Polly — Oh dear, if I had only let Polly stay with that woman she would have a clean bed and — "

Miriam grasped her sister's hand tightly. "Polly is better off with you, even here. And it won't be long. We will think of something."

"And you, Miriam?" asked Susanna, holding fast to Miriam's hand and looking earnestly into the girl's face. "To think that we had to leave you alone! Can you manage by yourself in that room?"

"Of course I can, Susanna. I have a dress for Madame to work on, and the tailor is so busy he's glad of my help. Truly, you don't need to worry about me. 'Tis you and the children. How can you bear this horrible place?"

Susanna's face, pale and frighteningly thin, was curiously serene. In the murky light of the cell her eyes were luminous.

" 'Tis all right, Miriam," she answered quietly. "If only the children do not get sick. For me, it does not matter. I can stand anything now, anything, so long as James is with me again."

Miriam could barely keep from running as the guard led her back through the jail. When the heavy door swung open, she flung herself forward into the clean sunlight and stood gasping as though she had escaped some indescribable horror. Pierre was still there, though for the moment he did not notice her, being engaged in a lively game of dice with the sentry. He looked up, grinned, pocketed the dice, and joined her.

"Was it worth all the fuss?" he inquired. "You look as though you'd seen a ghost."

"They are ghosts — those people in there. Pierre, it is a dreadful place — unclean — oh, horrible!"

Pierre shrugged. "They should be smart enough to stay out of it, then."

"But do they really deserve to be there? Maybe there are others like Susanna and James. And little children! I can't bear to think of it."

"You are a softhearted little thing, in spite of that temper," he commented. "Those people aren't worth your pity. Your sister, of course, that is different. Something should be done about her."

She seized this opening to explain about the letter

James had written. Pierre's face darkened.

"See here, my *petite*," he said finally. "I am not going to get mixed up in this business of English prisoners. And I haven't the influence you seem to think. In fact, I am pretty generally out of favor in the regiment, thanks to their fool regulations."

When they reached the tailor shop, however, he reconsidered. "One thing I can do," he admitted. "I know a good Indian runner who can be persuaded to take your letter to Albany. He owes me his skin. He can be trusted to bring back the money, which is more than you could say for a lot of them. There now, that's more like it," he added as Miriam's face went radiant. "Now will you take the weight of the world off those pretty shoulders? I shall get a carriage, and we will drive out along the river."

And this time she went.

With the letter on its way to Albany, Miriam's heart was somewhat lightened. She finished the dress for Madame Du Quesne, and the tailor, flooded with orders from the French soldiers that swarmed the streets, gave her odd jobs that filled her hours. Except for the thought of Susanna she was not unhappy. Often, remembering her sister, she was ashamed at how all her senses responded to the warm pulse of summertime. Perhaps it was the cups of chocolate and the odd dainties that were urged on her by Pierre.

Once he even arrived with a whole roast chicken wrapped in a napkin! Perhaps his very coming had answered a deeper hunger, for in spite of herself she found that she was constantly waiting for his unpredictable visits. His stride on the pavement outside her window, his mocking boastful voice made her breath come faster.

He did not mention again meeting his friends. In fact she could not help noticing that he was careful to avoid any place where they might be. They drove together along the river road in the dusk, or lingered at the table under the friendly eye of the tavern owner's wife. Miriam's role was very easy: she had only to listen. Pierre never tired of boasting of his exploits in the forest, of his beloved canoe, of the long journeys through winding river courses to the wealth of furs that waited in the unending country to the west. He loved to tell of his grandfather, seventy years old, but still the greatest *coureur* of them all, who could paddle the most dangerous rapids, endure the longest portage, and outsing and outdrink every trader in the West.

Listening, Miriam's imagination was stirred, her pioneer blood beat faster at the thought of the wild unexplored country. She would watch Pierre, totally unaware of her own shining eyes and parted lips. But sometimes he would fall silent, and then she would look away, unable to meet the half-taunting, half-caressing stare that rested on her as perceptibly as a touch. She was never really at ease with him. Always, behind his laughter, she glimpsed the lurking shadow of Mehkoa.

"What a silly goose I am," she would scold herself afterwards, when Pierre had gone, "to let a little flattery go to my head like this." Then in the silence of the room she would get out Phineas Whitney's letter, unfold it carefully, and read the scholarly lines again.

"Phineas Whitney is worth a dozen of him," she would remind herself. "And besides, Pierre may never come again." But even as she said it, something within her was listening and waiting, and the words on the sheet of paper were dim as an echo from a long long distance.

CHAPTER 20

THE WEATHER was unseasonably hot. Miriam worked steadily through the bright days, for the tailor turned over to her capable fingers more and more of the time-consuming details he disliked. The poorly ventilated room became stifling; the woolen homespun dress was intolerable and no longer respectable. Miriam was compelled to spend a portion of her wages on a length of cheap calico for a dress for herself. There was little pleasure either in the sewing or the wearing. The coarse, flimsy material was scarcely suited to high fashion, so she decided on a copy of the simple sacque she had made for the party at Number Four. She hoped that the color might please Pierre.

With a corner of her mind ever alert for his coming, she was working a buttonhole with painstaking care when the tailor called to her that a gentleman was waiting. To her surprise, it was not Pierre, but an erect, heavily braided footman who stood just inside the door of the shop. He carried a summons, he an-

228

nounced, for Miriam Willard to appear at once at the Governor's residence.

Hurrying beside him along the street, Miriam's thoughts zigzagged from hope to fear. Was her appeal to the Governor on behalf of Susanna and James to be granted at last? Or was it her turn now to be thrown into that fearsome jail?

She was familiar with the handsome stone Château De Vaudreuil overlooking the Quai, where the Governor of New France, who officially resided in Quebec, spent a portion of his time each year. The footman led her along a paved garden walk, through a rear doorway, and up a flight of stairs into a sun-filled sitting room.

"It is the English prisoner you sent for, my lady."

It was not the Governor she had come to see, but the Governor's lady. The Marquise De Vaudreuil reclined against a satin pillow on a chaise longue. She was a diminutive woman, with ivory pallor, small finely chiseled features, delicate wrists, and slender, white, blue-veined hands. Her voice was light and cool.

"Come in, my dear. I had not expected to find you so young."

Miriam curtsied and moved a few steps nearer.

"I have sent for you to do some work for me. An acquaintance here in Montreal, Madame Du Quesne, has confided to me, very unwillingly, where she and her daughter obtained their beautiful gowns. I should like to have you make one for me."

Miriam's knees went weak with surprise and relief. "I should be very happy to do so, my lady," she stammered.

"I am curious," the Marquise went on. "How did you come to learn dressmaking? I have never heard that the English colonies were famous for their fashion. You studied in Boston, perhaps?"

"I have never seen the Boston fashions," Miriam admitted. "Nor have I ever studied at all. I like to look at dresses, and I love the feel of the cloth. I think all I really have is patience."

"Imagination too, I should judge," said the Marquise, smiling. "You will need it to make me look presentable. I have grown so thin. Everything suitable that comes from France is far too large for me. Can you begin at once?"

"Oh yes, my lady."

The woman studied the girl's eager face. "How pretty you are," she said lightly. "But so thin, as thin as I am, *n'est-ce pas?* I shall have to try to fatten you, as they are always trying to do to me. Where do you live, my dear?"

"I have a room behind the shop of Monsieur Jacques, the tailor."

"You had best work here during the day. There is a small room at the end of the hall where the light is good. Come, I shall show you. I have had some bolts of cloth sent in for us to choose from."

So began another change in that year of bewildering changes. Every morning Miriam left the tailor shop, hastened to the Château, and settled herself for a day's work in the airy room where the sunshine poured in upon gleaming folds of satin. Never before had she had such beautiful goods to work with. The heavy, glossy weight sliding through her fingers was delicious. When she raised her eyes, she could watch the sails of the little boats on the St. Lawrence.

In the middle of the morning the Marquise would send for her. Beside the chaise longue would be set a silver tray with a little pot of fragrant chocolate, a china cup thin as an eggshell, and a plate of soft white rolls. "Drink a little more," the Marquise would urge. "Then they will tell my husband that the tray went back empty. It pleases him to think I am eating."

With her thoughtfulness the gentle Marquise met a much deeper need than the girl's ravenous young appetite. Her light, petal-like touch brushed away the hard shell that protected Miriam's bruised spirit. Gradually Miriam began to sense that the defiant pride, which had shielded her through so many battles this past year, was not needed in this place. Wary

231

at first, too ready for the biting word that never came, she slowly began to feel for this woman an admiration close to reverence. To win the Marquise's quiet smile of approval, Miriam worked as she had never known she could, grateful now even for the sharp eye of Madame Du Quesne which had trained her fingers to exactness.

In spite of the work, her strained nerves relaxed in the serenity and order of the Château. Her eager mind, which had led her to acquire in the Du Quesne household a smattering of fashion and fine living, began to absorb from this place a different kind of knowledge. Watching the exquisite Marquise, she became aware of the sharp corners of her own inexperience. For the first time her blunt New England speech seemed less a matter for pride. To speak with both sincerity and grace was not, she saw now, impossible. Also, she was learning to curb her impatience.

From the first day here Miriam had hoped that this unexpected entry into the Governor's household would provide an opportunity to speak for Susanna and James. Yet so far the opening had not come. Charming as the Marquise was to her, the distance between them was great. Moreover, it seemed unthinkable to intrude upon that flowerlike sweetness any hint of ugliness or suffering. She had yet to discover the strength beneath that delicate surface.

She was in the sitting room, fitting the nearly finished dress, when the door opened and a gentleman entered. Miriam scrambled to her feet for a curtsy. The fine stiff brocaded coat, the deep lace ruffles, and the impressive white wig could grace only the Governor himself. He turned toward her briefly, a face with clean-cut, rather too sharp features, a long thin nose, and finely modeled mouth and chin.

"I thought you would be resting, my dear Charlotte," he addressed his wife reproachfully.

"I have been resting all the morning," she assured him. "But my dress must be fitted. Do you like it, François? I meant it to surprise you."

"It is very becoming. But then, you always look charming to me. Do not keep her standing too long, girl," he added, glancing at Miriam.

His wife reached up to touch his cheek lightly. "I am not tired at all," she said fondly. "You must not coddle me so!"

All at once there came before Miriam a memory of her brother James, stooping in the forest to hoist the wicker basket that held Susanna. Why should this elegant pair call to mind those ragged figures? There had been something, a wordless sharing, a fleeting thing of the spirit, that flashed between them. It lingered in the air after the Marquis had gone, as palpable as a fragrance.

"We can stop now and try the dress again later, if you like," Miriam suggested.

"Yes, the standing tires me, though I did not wish my husband to know. He is overanxious about me. You see, I caught the fever while we were in New Orleans."

"New Orleans!" exclaimed Miriam. "Isn't that a very great distance from here?"

"An unthinkable distance," sighed the Marquise. "And so hot in the summer. And the snakes! I could never learn to hide my fear of them. But the flowers were beautiful. My husband was governor of Louisiana for three years."

The words were spoken so lightly, almost indifferently, yet Susanna was close to Miriam again. "You speak like my sister," she said impulsively.

"You have a sister?"

"She went with her husband too. I know she loved Massachusetts, where they lived before. But she went with him to the farthest settlement in New Hampshire, where she knew well enough what might happen."

"Did something happen?"

It was the opening she had not dared to hope would come so soon. Under that compassionate gaze, Miriam plunged in, forgetting the careful speech she had prepared for when her chance might come. She had only intended to speak about the jail. But the thought of Susanna possessed her. She wanted this woman to understand her sister, who had endured that dreadful morning at Charlestown, who had given birth in the wilderness, and stayed behind alone in the village of St. Francis. The Marquise sat listening, her eyes dwelling gently on the girl's ardent face.

"You are very fond of your sister, aren't you?" she commented. "It is a pity that you should be separated."

"The jail is such a dreadful place," Miriam went on. "There are rats and dirt, and the dampness and smell are horrible. Oh my lady, would you be willing? Could you speak for my sister? I would do anything, anything I could in return."

The Marquise was thoughtful. "I do not understand the matter of prisoners," she said at last. "My husband does not wish me to concern myself with public affairs at all. But I shall see what I can do."

Miriam could not answer, yet the tears that flooded her eyes spoke her thanks eloquently. The Marquise leaned forward and touched the girl's hand.

"Let us look at the bolts of cloth again," she suggested. "I have not decided what we shall make next."

Miriam understood that the distressing subject was closed. The Marquise fingered the goods thoughtfully.

"This flowered pattern is cool and pretty," she said, picking up a fine sprigged muslin. "But too young for me, I think. It was surely meant for a girl. Take it and make something for yourself."

"That lovely piece! It is far too grand for me," Miriam gasped.

"It is quite a simple thing," smiled the Marquise. "Take it, please. It is just suited to you."

For the rest of the day, while her fingers worked on one dress, Miriam's mind was fashioning another. The joy of having a new piece of goods, all of her own, to plan and cut just as she chose! At last, hugging the material close to her, she hastened home along the street at such a pace that she almost bumped into Hortense before she recognized her.

"I'm so thankful," beamed Hortense, when she had learned of the new work. "I have tried at the tailor shop twice, and I was worried about you. Yes, everyone speaks well of the Governor's wife. They say she is better than he deserves, in fact. What a lucky thing to have happened! But I was coming to remind you of the wedding. You promised, you know. It is only three days away."

"Please, Miriam," she begged as Miriam hesitated. "I want my friends to be there. You see, we must have a specially happy wedding. Jules has been called into the regiment. Any day now he will have to march out with them, and who knows how long he will be gone?"

Miriam promised. She would work every spare moment of daylight and have the new dress to wear. And when Pierre came again, how astonished he would be!

The material spread across her bed like a field of flowers, Miriam set to work. But the rapture she had anticipated suddenly deserted her. Instead, a nagging memory tormented her. Such a small thing. If she had not run into Hortense she would never in the world have thought of it again. But now, wherever she looked, there was Hortense, touching a yellow satin gown with a timid finger, and in her ears was a wistful voice, "I wish that just once in my life, for my wedding, I could have a beautiful dress to wear."

Oh, why did I have to think of it! She struggled inwardly with herself. Why did I have to meet her today, before I had it cut out and started?

The girl of last winter would not have hesitated.

But in these last months the old defenses had worn thin. They were not proof against the memories that plagued her. She could see a pair of merry black eyes twinkling over a red blanket held up to shield her. She could see an anxious figure hurrying along the snowy street to find two banished women and take them home. Always Hortense had given. Now, unexpectedly, here in her hands was something to give, a perfect wedding present.

"She is just about my height, but much stockier," she told herself, firmly stamping down her own anguished protests. "I had better do it fast, before I change my mind."

Every persistent doubt was silenced three days later when she stood in the parish church and watched Hortense take her marriage vows. The memory of Hortense's astonishment and joy was like a precious jewel held concealed in her hand. Holding such wealth, it did not matter how she looked to the others. Even more, in a way she had not foreseen, the gift had brought her inside the circle. Never, when she had lived in their house, had she felt one with the family as she did today. A warm current of affection linked her with her friend's mother, radiant with pride in her eldest daughter, with the little girls, whose adoration shone in their scrubbed faces, even with Jules, whose eyes dwelt on his bride with unconcealed worship.

Hortense's round face was touched with beauty as she spoke the solemn words. It was the first wedding Miriam had ever attended. She had come into this alien church reluctantly, almost fearfully. But with the happy new warmth melting her strangeness, she was moved beyond any expectation by the chanting voices. Though she could not understand it, the ritual of the mass held her enthralled. Never again would she shudder with distrust as she passed the churches of Montreal, knowing now that they contained only this reverence and beauty.

CHAPTER 2I

Two DAYS after Hortense's wedding
the militia was alerted. Word spread that English
troops were marching on Fort Duquesne, a western
outpost which the French had no intention of aban-
doning. Hearing the news, walking through streets
astir with soldiers, Miriam's first thought was of Hortense, who must see her bridegroom march away so
soon.

It was suppertime when she returned to the tailor's
shop and saw to her astonishment the familiar Du
Quesne carriage almost filling the narrow street in
front of her door. The footman climbed down as he
saw her coming and judging by his ill-humor, he must
have been waiting for some time.

"I was told by Madame Du Quesne to bring you
at once. Get in quickly. There will be trouble enough
for this delay."

At the Du Quesne residence a state of emergency
was apparent. The muslin dress that had fitted Felicité so perfectly on May Day could not be persuaded

to fasten tonight. Within the next two hours a trouble-some alteration must be completed. No one inquired whether or not Miriam had had supper. She was set to work at once in the well-remembered white and blue room.

Felicité hurried back from her own dinner too impatient to stay far from Miriam's side. She was much too excited to remember the old grudge that lay between them. She had to talk to someone, and her silvery chatter was as breathless as ever.

"The most divine man, truly, Miriam, the most hand-some man you ever saw! Think of it, so young, and captain of that great ship! Can't you pull the waist just a tiny bit tighter? Oh dear, if only I hadn't eaten that whole box of meringues! But all the men keep bringing me these boxes, straight from France, and I just can't leave them alone!"

The moment Madame Du Quesne entered, all illusion of the old days vanished. Felicité knew enough to keep silent. Miriam might have been invisible for all the notice they took of her. Madame was out of sorts.

"I'm not sure you are being wise, Felicité," she said once, without even as much caution as she would have observed before the kitchen maid. "We know nothing at all about this young captain."

"Oh, Maman!" Felicité protested. "I'm not going to

marry him! His ship sails back in a week or so and I'll never see him again. Besides, I'll be settled and dull soon enough."

"Certain people," Madame reminded her meaningfully, "cannot be provoked too far. I hope you know what you are doing."

Felicité's curls tossed. "Certain people have been much too independent lately," she answered. "You leave that to me, Maman. I know exactly what I am doing."

When Felicité had finally tripped out of the room in the newly fitted dress to join her handsome captain, Miriam gathered together her thread and scissors and went on her way home. Madame was nowhere to be seen, and it was futile to wait for any payment tonight. The street was dark as she hurried nervously along, and she shrank against the wall as a noisy group of soldiers and girls crowded her off the pavement. They were well past her when one of the group glanced back, stared for a moment, and abruptly left the others. As he came closer, she recognized Pierre, his uniform pulled carelessly open at the throat, his black tricorne teetering on the back of his rumpled head.

"Miriam? Is it you? *Parbleu,* girl! What are you thinking of to be out on the street at this hour?"

"I am on my way home," Miriam faltered. "I did not realize it was so late."

"Don't you know that the troops are marching in the morning? Every sober citizen in Montreal will stay inside and lock the door tonight."

"Madame had some work for me to do. It is just finished."

"Drat the woman! What sort of work, that couldn't wait?"

"I have told you I am a dressmaker. Felicité's gown needed to be fitted in a hurry. I am going home directly now."

"*Un moment!* This gown — why must it be fitted in such a hurry?"

"Why — " All at once she saw how she had blundered. Would she never learn to hold her tongue?

"To be worn tonight, by any chance?"

"Pierre, I don't — "

"Answer me!" His fingers bruised her arm.

"Yes, she wore it somewhere tonight."

"The little weasel! Sick in bed with a headache, was she? On my last night!"

The black anger gathered in him like a terrifying wave.

"Please, Pierre! If you will let me by. I must get home." As she tried to pull away from his grasp he noticed her again.

"I will see you home," he said automatically, hardly aware of what he said.

243

"You don't need to. If you will just let me — "

"Stop your chattering and come along!"

She hurried to keep step with him, thankful to be moving in the right direction. She had merely her own clumsiness to blame for this, she knew. She had been fearful ever since she had met Pierre of provoking the violence that lurked beneath that gay surface. Tonight she was too tired to cope with it. She was impatient when, after a few steps, he halted again.

"Wait. I have thought of something."

With his grip on her arm she waited uneasily while he weighed this something in his mind. Once again, in the darkness, his face reminded her of an Indian's. His eyes, glinting under lowered lids, looked reckless and crafty.

"So you work for Madame Du Quesne," he said at last, in a deceptively casual voice. "I might have put two and two together. My mother has been in a frenzy to know where those new gowns have been coming from."

"I shouldn't have let it slip out. I promised not to tell."

"Well, my good mother is going to find out, right now. We will stop and tell her, and from now on, my little seamstress, I promise you more business than you can handle."

"Not tonight, Pierre. Tomorrow morning, perhaps. No one wants to talk about dressmaking tonight."

"I want to talk about it," Pierre said roughly. "Come along!"

Was there no way to escape him? Was he drunk like the other soldiers whose tipsy shouts filled the streets? Miriam was too inexperienced to tell. And why this talk of dressmaking when he could barely hold in leash his jealous fury? To cross him now would be foolhardy. Better to humor him and, if she could, deliver him safely into his mother's hands and make her escape.

Indeed, she had little choice. He was hurrying her till her breath came in tight gasps, along the moonlit street, down a garden path, into a side doorway.

"Pierre — I am sure this is not your house! I will not — " Too late she understood his trickery. The door opened directly into a long drawing room. There was a dazzle of lights and voices, and the sound of violins. Behind her she heard the door click shut. She stood frozen. The room whirled in a great colored pinwheel, and a roaring in her ears shut out the music. Her forehead felt cold. She must actually have lost her balance, for she was aware of pain in her arm as Pierre held her to her feet. The faintness passed. As her sight cleared, two figures emerged from the mass and came toward them, a woman as haughty as a queen, and an elderly man with heavy snow-white hair and a black velvet coat. The woman's voice was sharp.

"Pierre! What are you doing here in those clothes?"

245

"My dear Maman, where is our hostess? I have brought a distinguished guest to her party!"

"Pierre! You have been drinking!"

"The idea! Maman, Grandpère, allow me to introduce my guest!"

Madame's horrified gaze swept over the trembling girl. "Who is this girl? Pierre, have you lost your mind? Felicité is here!"

"So I understand!"

Madame Laroche came closer. "Hush, Pierre! I will not tolerate this. You must get away before the others see you."

But the damage was done. In the whole long room there was suddenly not a voice. The roaring began again in Miriam's ears, and from a great distance she heard a man's voice, deep and kind.

"My dear mademoiselle," said the man in the black velvet coat, and incredulously she saw that he was bowing to her, "allow me to bid you welcome. But I did not catch your name?"

"Willard," she forced her lips to shape the word. "Miriam Willard." And with the name the whirling pinwheel slowed to a stop. "Willard," she repeated, half aloud, and it was like a draught of water, cold and strengthening. Her shoulders straightened, her head lifted. She could hear the music again.

Pierre turned to her. "Shall we dance?" he asked mockingly.

Miriam drew a steadying breath. It was like that moment on the shore at St. Francis, when she had known that she must run the gantlet. A pathway cleared in the room, and they waited to see what she would do. She glimpsed Madame Du Quesne, and Felicité, her face shocked to blankness like a painted doll's.

Suddenly a gust of anger shook her, a fury as deadly as Pierre's. Who were these people anyway, these be-ruffled, sophisticated creatures who behaved like savages? Not one of them had ever faced an Indian gantlet. Not one of them had ever done an honest day's work in return for the food that ruined their

247

fashionable figures. She was through with standing in awe of them, of meekly holding silent, and flattening herself invisible against muddy walls. Never again, no matter what it cost her, would she wait humbly for their favor. She despised them, every one of them!

Her head went up. Two brilliant spots of color flared in her cheeks. Deliberately she turned and laid a hand on Pierre's shoulder. "If you wish," she said icily. "By all means, let us dance."

Her feet, in the leather sandals, had not forgotten the minuet. The slender calico figure moved with grace among the satins. Amid powdered curls, the smooth chestnut-red wings of her hair glowed like candlelight. Any ripple of amusement that might have begun was shriveled by the blazing scorn in her gray eyes. As the dance ended she faced a completely sobered partner.

"Now," she demanded imperiously, "you will kindly see that I get home at once."

At the door the elder Monsieur Laroche intercepted them. "My grandson scarcely deserves the honor of seeing you home," he said. "I have ordered a carriage for you." He bowed very low over her hand. "We have been honored, mademoiselle. You are a very beautiful and gallant young lady. If your English soldiers show half your spirit in battle, we French will have no easy victory."

CHAPTER 22

ONLY A SHORT TIME, it seemed, after Miriam had thrown herself into bed, drained of ability even to think further, she was aroused by a spatter of pebbles against her window.

"Miriam!" It was Pierre's voice, cautiously half raised. The hail of pebbles was repeated. He would wake the tailor's wife with this racket. Climbing on a chair to peer out the high window, she could just make out his figure in the dimness of early morning.

"Pierre!" she whispered. "What are you thinking of? Go away!"

"I have got to see you. Let me in, Miriam, will you please?"

"You know I can't do that. And I don't want to see you or hear you."

"I don't deserve it, I know that. But I must talk to you."

"Not at this hour!"

"We assemble at daybreak. I can't wait till a decent time. Come out and talk to me here, then. There is something I must say to you."

"No! Go away!"

"Look here, my girl." Pierre's voice lost its caution. "Either you let me in or come out here and listen, or I'll shout what I have to say so loud that every soul in this street will hear me!"

"Oh, wait a minute!" Miriam agreed in exasperation. Climbing down from the chair she hastily drew on the calico dress, pulled a muslin cap over her tousled hair, and crept soundlessly through the shop into the street.

"*Bon!* I knew you would come. What a girl! Even at this hour you look beautiful!"

She drew back from his outstretched hands. "Whatever you have to say, Pierre, say it quickly."

"You will not make it easy for me, *n'est-ce pas?* Never mind. I'll get down on my knees to you here on the pavestones if you like. Will you forgive me for last night, Miriam?"

When she did not answer, he hurried on. "It was an unspeakable thing to do. I knew it the moment I came to my senses. But I lost my head there on the street. I can't see now why I ever thought she was worth it!"

"You don't need to explain. It doesn't matter in the least."

"It mattered last night, and you know it. You can

call me anything you like. You should have heard my
grandfather! Though when it comes to losing your
temper, you must admit you haven't much to say!"

"No. I admit I was angry."

"Angry! *Parbleu!* You were magnificent! Not a
woman in Montreal could have done it!"

"Hush, Pierre! Everyone will hear you!"

"Very well, but am I forgiven? Think, Miriam, you can't let a man go off to battle without being forgiven! Here I am, marching off to die for King and country —"

"Oh stop it, Pierre!" Always he somehow made her laugh, no matter how unwillingly. "All right. You are forgiven. Now, please, will you go away?"

"Not yet. I haven't said what I came to say. Will you marry me, Miriam?"

It was the last thing she had expected. She could only stare at him.

"Don't answer yet. I know what you think. You think I am still mad at Felicité, but that is not so. How I could even have looked at her, with a girl like you right under my nose! When I saw you standing there last night, with your head in the air! Such spirit! Such fire! I could have knelt down and asked you right there, in front of all of them!"

"Pierre — I —"

"I would marry you today if I could. But this cursed campaign will take a month or more. The day I come home we will arrange it. I will build the finest house in Montreal. Why don't you say something? Are you not pleased?"

"You can't mean this, Pierre. You will regret it tomorrow," Miriam answered, striving hard to hold to her own common sense. "You have said over and over how you had to be free, how you would never be tied down as long as you lived."

"Wait a minute! Who is talking of being tied down? I am still a *coureur*, make no mistake about that. But every *coureur* wants to have a wife to come home to."

"Is that what you want of me? To wait here in Montreal while you are off for a year at a time?"

"But what else does a trader's wife expect?"

A queer trembling had taken possession of Miriam. The spark that had been lighted the first time she heard the rollicking song of the *coureur de bois* flamed now to give her courage. Sometimes, in the loneliness of her room, she had allowed herself to dream of marriage to Pierre. Always she had pictured herself beside him, sharing the excitement and the danger of the wild unexplored country and the endless shining riverways.

"A wife could go with you!" she spoke impetuously. "Women have traveled through the wilderness before and lived on the frontiers!"

Pierre threw back his head and roared. "What a girl! Imagine Felicité suggesting such a thing! But you have the wrong idea, my love. I am no settler. I am a trader, and believe me, there is no room for a woman in a *voyageur's* canoe!"

His laughter hurt her. " 'Tis not much of a marriage you have to offer then," she said in disappointment.

Pierre was affronted now. "There's plenty of others who've thought I had something to offer. What do you want, anyway? Why, I can give you dresses that will make the womens' eyes pop out! With your beauty I could make you the talk of New France. What a pair we would make! As my wife you'd be second to no one in Montreal — or Quebec either, for that matter!"

Miriam stared up at him for a moment. "Pierre, this isn't a joke to you? I'm beginning to believe you are serious."

"But certainly I am serious. Believe me, Miriam, I have never before asked a girl to be my wife. What more can I say?"

Surely there was something more he could say if he chose. Perhaps it was the unromantic hour, or the public place, or the sense of hurry as the city began to wake and stir that prevented the word she waited for.

"If you are serious," she said slowly, "then I thank you. But I can't decide now, not this very minute like this. Will you wait till you come back, and give me time to think about it?"

Pierre laughed confidently. "Think all you like, my love," he agreed. "And here's something to think about." He pulled her abruptly against the knobby uniform and kissed her triumphantly. The muslin cap slid off onto the pavement.

"*Au revoir*," he said gaily. "We will get this battle over with in a hurry. They had better not keep me long away from my redheaded bride!"

Later, from the window of the Château, Miriam watched the troops on the parade ground below, as they passed in review before the Governor. From that distance she could not distinguish Pierre's face under the tricorne hat, but his arrogant swinging stride was unmistakable. He and his companions made a colorful picture, with their white uniforms faced with scarlet and purple and yellow, their black-gaitered legs stepping in unison. Above them the white banners flaunted the gold lilies of France.

The roll of the drums stirred Miriam's senses. It was impossible to imagine these glittering ranks engaged in actual battle, and the thought of war held little meaning for her. It was only when she saw, following the regular troops, the row on row of Indians in war paint that she felt a twinge of uneasiness. There were so many Indians, three times as many as the French soldiers. What part could they play in defending a French fort?

It was well that the Marquise left her to herself to-day. Her fingers were clumsy with the needle, and many times her work dropped neglected in her lap while she lost herself in a frenzy of dizzy imaginings. The finest house in Montreal, he had boasted! She gazed around her. What would it be like to walk all day on such soft carpets, to have the right to touch every piece of furniture and silver and china and know that it was her own? And to choose from these lavish bolts of materials the clothes that would make her beautiful? Yet all day long, behind these dazzling thoughts, there was a question she did not want to answer, that, thankfully, she would not be forced to answer just yet. There was still a little time.

After the astonishment of the past hours, she was scarcely able to be surprised when that evening the white-haired Monsieur Laroche called on her. Her first impression of him was instantly confirmed. No one could help liking this vigorous, confident man, with his handsome weather-beaten face that still bore the stamp of nobility. She could feel no resentment when he came directly to the point.

"When my grandson left this morning," he said, "I was quite sure he was going to ask you to marry him."

Miriam's blush was answer enough.

"I am glad to know it. If he had not, I intended to do it for him now."

Miriam stared at him. "You mean — you approve?"

"I had about given up hope that I would ever find a wife suitable for my grandson. Last night I saw that he had found her for himself. I had not given him credit for so much good sense."

"But I am English!"

"French — English — it is all the same to me. It is the woman who matters. You, my dear, have exactly what he needs, beauty, intelligence, and the spirit to hold him. I trust you have accepted him?"

While Miriam searched for the right word to say, he studied her shrewdly.

"Surely you are not holding last night's bad manners against him. The boy is young. I had the same quick temper when I was his age. That is why he needs a girl like you who will not give in to his tantrums. But you are too fine a person to let one mistake keep you from a husband like Pierre."

Miriam still had no answer, yet she felt instinctively that she could speak honestly to this man. No wonder Pierre adored his grandfather. There was no question about the love and pride that lay behind this frank appeal.

"What is it, mademoiselle?" he urged, his black eyes both kind and puzzled. "Perhaps I seem overproud of Pierre. But I have raised him from a small boy. He is a true *coureur*. No one can outwit him, and he is afraid of nothing. He is lively company and generous. And I have observed that here in Montreal the ladies do not find him undesirable. Why is it that you do not favor my Pierre?"

257

"I do like him, very much," Miriam answered, wanting to return his frankness. "But I am not sure. I am afraid that to Pierre I am just something he has taken a fancy to, like another ornament to put in this fine house he is going to build. To sit there alone, just waiting for when he chooses to come home — should there not be more to a marriage than that?"

He nodded wisely. "Ah yes, you are very young, and romantic. But you must also be sensible. Let us be quite honest, you and I. No *coureur* ever made a devoted husband. His true heart is always in the forest. But in the long run there are more practical things to consider. Pierre has a fortune of his own, and he will someday inherit all that I possess as well. Do not demand too much, my dear. Pierre's wife will be a very fortunate woman."

CHAPTER **23**

U NDER THE BURNING July sun the city
waited. Miriam could not escape the growing tension.
In the tailor shop men talked constantly of war. In
the streets there was a heaviness in the air, like the
charged stillness in the path of a distant storm. At
the Château the servants scurried to avoid the impatient step of the Governor, and even the Marquise
was often preoccupied and anxious.

One morning, looking up from her work, Miriam
was awed by the sight of a great ship, white sails filled,
moving along the river like a queen, flying the gold
lilies of France. Later in the day, in the parade ground
beneath her window, there was a review of troops.
They had come from France under General Dieskau,
she learned, and they intended to make short work
of the fracas. Very different they appeared from the
swaggering local militia, these rigidly disciplined
ranks, wheeling and advancing in perfect unison. Yet
even this evidence could not make the war a reality
for Miriam. The conflict was too remote, the issues

at stake too vast. All the uneasiness of the great city seemed to be only a reflection of the tumult in her own mind.

Every passing day brought nearer the moment when her decision must be made. Or had the decision already been made? Both Pierre and his grandfather had taken her hesitation to be nothing more than coy acceptance. She had only to keep silent and every costly thing she had learned to value would be hers. Then why did the thought of Pierre's return set her heart thudding with dread? Since May Day, no, since the first moment she had seen him on the street of Montreal, he had possessed her thoughts, even her dreams. The other image, of Phineas Whitney, was dim and indistinct, a man whom a different girl had loved in a time almost forgotten. Surely Phineas could not be the cause of this uncertainty. What was it she instinctively distrusted? Why, when the future promised to fulfill every dream, did she still feel a sense of loss, as though she had reached for some priceless thing and found her hands still empty?

She came one morning into the sitting room to find the Marquise smiling eagerly. The Governor stood nearby, tapping with slender nervous fingers on a polished tabletop.

"Come in, my dear," the Marquise greeted her. "The Governor has something to tell you."

The Governor coldly acknowledged her curtsy. "The Marquise has been begging me for some weeks," he began, "to look into the matter of your sister and her family. It is a time when I can scarcely afford to be concerned with trivial affairs, but I can seldom refuse my wife. I have ascertained that some money has arrived by messenger from Albany. Nowhere near enough, you understand, to discharge the debts Captain Johnson has incurred here in Montreal. But because of my good wife, I have decided to be exceedingly lenient. The Captain and his family will be released tomorrow morning."

He raised a hand to prevent her interrupting thanks.

"I have no intention of releasing the Captain to fight against us. At any rate, it is out of the question for him to return overland to the English colonies. I could not guarantee him safe conduct for a single day. There is one course open. There has been much fighting in Europe, and many French prisoners are now held in England. A ship leaves here tomorrow for Quebec, and from there for France. By special agreement it will stop at the port of Plymouth in England for the exchange of prisoners of war. The Captain and his wife and children, and you yourself, will be included in this exchange. I have given orders for him to be conducted straight to the ship at six o'clock tomorrow morning and you will meet him there. From England you will no doubt be able to secure passage back to your colonies."

Since he disdainfully rebuffed her gratitude, Miriam steadied her voice and tried to express her thanks with dignity. After her husband had left the room, the Marquise spoke gently.

"It was a pleasure to do it, my dear. I know how troubled you have been about your sister."

"We shall be so grateful to you, my lady, as long as we live," Miriam told her. "Oh, I can scarcely believe it, that Susanna is free to go home, after all she has suffered."

"Yes. She is free. I should like to meet your sister, I think, but there will be no chance for that."

Miriam hesitated. "We have never been on a ship," she confessed. "I am a little frightened when I think of that great distance."

"It is not so far nowadays," the Marquise assured her. "The new ships make the voyage in a month or less. But I have been wondering about you. You have learned to speak French so fluently. Are you determined to go with your sister? I should be so happy to take you with me to Quebec when we return."

Miriam stared at her in surprise.

"I confess it is selfish of me to suggest it. You are by far the best dressmaker I have ever had. But I think you would not be unhappy in Quebec, and, who

262

knows, perhaps you might find a young man who could persuade you to make it your home."

Miriam, looking down at the rug, felt her color rising under the keen eyes that studied her face.

"I have suspected lately," said the Marquise softly, "that there might already be such a young man. Is that true?"

"Yes, my lady."

"A young habitant, perhaps? And he has asked you to marry him? What do you really want to do, my dear?"

Miriam still could not meet the older woman's gaze. Suppose she were to tell the truth? Would the Marquise be outraged at the thought of an English prisoner presuming to marry a French nobleman? Yet it would be so wonderful a relief to find someone who would listen and advise.

"I am not sure," she began, searching for words.

"When I was your age, I was sure," the Marquise answered, speaking almost to herself. "I would have gone anywhere in the world without a moment's hesitation. I know that people do not understand my husband. I know the things they say. But for me, all I ask still is to be able to stay beside him, or to go, wherever he needs me."

Miriam felt shut out again, baffled by that sureness she could not share. She could not confide in this woman, after all. Nor could she explain to Susanna, remembering her sister's eyes shining in the prison cell, and the steady voice saying, "I can stand anything, anything, so long as James is with me." Nor even to Hortense, who had given her whole heart into Jules's keeping. For all of them marriage seemed so simple a thing, so unquestioned. Why must it be, for her, so complicated by doubt and compromise?

"You must do what your own heart tells you," the Marquise said finally, taking the girl's hand in her own. "If you do not come tomorrow morning, I shall understand. God bless you, whatever you decide."

By evening Miriam determined that she must talk to someone. She could count on Hortense for a warm and affectionate listener, and when she left the Château at suppertime she walked along the river road to visit her friend.

Hortense, a neighbor informed her, was at her mother's house, so Miriam continued her walk to the familiar cottage, sure of a welcome. There she found everything unchanged, the same warm greeting, the happy clamor of the children, the taking for granted that she would share the evening meal of fish and vegetables. She was so far from being company now that the family bickering about the table was unchecked, and Alphonse did not escape a scolding when he slid into place after grace had been said.

"I was down on the wharf," he explained. "The ship from France is sailing in the morning. The sailors were climbing all over the rigging. How do they dare to go so high, Maman? What do they hold on to?"

Hortense's eyes flashed briefly toward Miriam. Did she suspect? Miriam wondered. So often those black eyes, childlike and dancing as they appeared, had the penetration to read her mind. But there was no chance for confidences here. After supper, on the road along the river, they could talk.

Is this the last time? Miriam wondered, looking from face to face. If she should sail in the morning, she would never see them again, never sit in this bright room that had been home to her. Yet if she stayed, in the fine house Pierre had promised her, would she still be welcome here, or would a strangeness come between them?

Suddenly, bursting in upon their meal, came the sound of churchbells. No stately Sabbath tolling it was, but a mad clamor, as though the hands that jerked the ropes could not wait for the bells to swing back. As they stared at each other with startled eyes, the floor beneath them rocked with a thunderous blast.

"The cannon!" gasped Hortense. She pushed back her chair and leaped to her feet. "Come with me, Miriam — quick!"

In the road Hortense set a pace that Miriam could scarcely match. Alphonse dashed past them, his brown legs kicking up spurts of dust.

Inside the gates of Montreal there was tumult. Doors were flung open, and children and bareheaded women rushed into the street. In the middle of the road neighbors hugged each other with tears streaming down their cheeks. Alphonse came dashing back to them, his eyes popping with excitement.

"It is over!" he shouted, choking for breath. "The battle is over! The English are beaten!"

"Are you sure?" Hortense demanded, catching him fiercely by the arm.

"The runners came back, a quarter-hour ago. One

of them is down there in the tavern." Jerking from his sister's grasp, he was off.

"Come!" ordered Hortense, and, bewildered, Miriam managed to stay at her heels.

There was no question what tavern Alphonse had meant. The door was mobbed with shouting men and boys trying to push their way inside. At the fringe a few daring women stood on tiptoe, craning their necks for a glimpse of the hero. He could barely be seen, through the open door, lifted high on a table, a weary grin flashing over a tankard of ale.

"You can't go in there, Hortense!" protested Miriam, seeing her friend's intent.

"Nonsense," said Hortense. "I can see that's only François Jobin. I've known him all my life. Let me in there!" she ordered, digging a forceful elbow into the nearest ribs.

"The dirty poachers!" someone was shouting. "They'll stay out of our beaver territory from now on!"

"By all the saints, that Braddock was one surprised general!" agreed the hero, wiping a froth of ale from his chin. Looking up, he spied the determined girl pushing toward him. "Look who comes here! My little friend Hortense! La, girl, you don't need to look like a ghost. Your man wasn't touched. Last I saw of him he was four steps ahead of the whole army in a fever to get back to his bride!"

There was a roar of laughter. Hortense turned back, her cheeks on fire. Yet she did not really mind. She did not even hear the rude jokes that set Miriam's ears tingling. Into her eyes had sprung such radiance that Miriam could not bear to look.

"Weren't many touched," the runner was continuing. "Five men killed, and a parcel of Indians. Not one of the officers was even nicked."

The question Miriam dared not ask was answered. Pierre too was hurrying back toward his bride. Yet she felt no rush of joy, only a cold quiver of dread, deep within her.

The boastful voice of the runner followed her through the door. "Caught them right in a trap, we did, before they even knew we were anywhere around. Those Indians know how to fight. They keep out of sight behind the trees. The stupid English farmers couldn't even see where to shoot at. They were firing every which way, killing off their own men. Dead bodies piled up five deep on the ground!" He took a deep draught and smacked his lips with satisfaction.

A wave of nausea swept over Miriam. These were Englishmen he was talking about! The English had been defeated! Impossible! It must be a lie! Never for one instant had she dreamed that this unreal war could mean defeat. Fear welled up in her. Englishmen, caught in a trap, shooting at an enemy they couldn't even see! Stupid English farmers, more handy with an axe and a plow than with a gun. Men like the ones she knew at Charlestown. Men she did know, perhaps! Oh God in heaven, she had never thought! Even her own father, it might be, or — Phineas Whitney!

In cold blackness she leaned against the plaster wall. All at once, so clear and close that she could almost touch him, his face had come back to her — the fine serious mouth, the steady blue eyes.

"Miriam, are you ill? Come away from this crowd!" Hortense was steadying her. She felt the fresh breeze from the river against her face. Gradually her heart slowed its pounding.

"Forgive me, Miriam," said Hortense softly. "I forgot it is not a time of gladness for you. You know that I am not happy because we won over your people. It is just for Jules. You understand?"

"Yes," Miriam answered with wonder. "I do understand. I never did before."

Phineas had come back to her! Pierre, marching back to the city, seemed a stranger compared to the closeness, the dearness of the memory that she had lost and that was now hers again. She had almost let go the priceless thing that had been hers all along. What was it Phineas had written? "Every hope of the future is meaningless unless I have faith that you and

I will share it together." How could she have forgotten? That was what she really wanted, a man she could wait for without a shadow of fear or doubt, knowing that at the end of waiting she would stand at his side, working with him, and sharing, and loving.

"Oh, Hortense," she burst out, "how I envy you! If only I could know that he is safe, and that someday I would see him again!"

Hortense studied her friend silently. "I think you are talking about an Englishman, not a Frenchman at all," she said, with her uncanny perception. "A man from your own country."

Miriam nodded. "You knew about Pierre?"

"I heard he had been seen with you. I knew that you would tell me someday, when you were ready."

"I came to tell you tonight. I didn't know what to do, and I wanted you to help me. But now, all of a sudden, I don't need to ask, I know! This is what you all have, you, and Susanna, and the Marquise!"

Hortense did not follow all this, but as usual she went straight to the heart of the matter.

"Then you mean to go away," she stated wistfully.

"You know about the ship too? Hortense, is there anything you don't hear about in this city?"

Hortense smiled. "I did not know about your Englishman. Now that I do know, I can let you go. I am so glad, Miriam, that there is someone waiting for you."

"Perhaps it will be too late. It will take such a long time, all the way to England and back. He may not wait so long. But no — I think he is like your Jules. I can trust him always. I will have to learn somehow to have faith, like you and Susanna. Oh Hortense, wish me well, please!"

"I will always wish you well, Miriam, whatever you do," Hortense answered. The two girls gazed at each other soberly.

"We will be enemies," said Hortense sadly.

Miriam threw her arms about her friend. "Oh no, Hortense! I could never be your enemy. You know that!"

"You and I, in our hearts, no. But your Englishman and my Jules, they are enemies. And there is so much hatred everywhere."

"There was a truce before. Perhaps there may be again. When I get home, I shall tell them, everyone I meet, what it is like here in Montreal. If they understand, they can't go on hating."

But she knew they would never understand. To the stern New Englanders Montreal was a place of wickedness, like the ancient cities of Sodom and Gomorrah. If they heard that it had been wiped from the earth with every soul it contained, they would accept such a fate as the just will of God. Oh, pray that no harm should come to this city that she had grown to love! Tears filled her eyes.

271

"I can't bear to say goodbye to you, Hortense!"

"Then let us not say it tonight," answered Hortense practically. "Let me stay with you tonight and help you to make ready, and tomorrow morning I will stand on the shore and wave to you. See, they are making ready to sail."

Their arms about each other's waists, the two girls stood for a moment, staring high above the rooftops at the masts that lifted against the evening sky. The sharp calls of the sailors in the rigging carried clearly through the summer twilight. In the morning those vast sails would be released to billow out and catch the wind. What would it be like to have no solid ground under one's feet, to hear only the howling wind, to strain one's eyes and see nothing but sky and water week after week? She shivered, yet at the same time her mind leaped ahead toward this new adventure.

"Whatever may lie between this day and our next meeting —" Phineas had written. A bloody war for him, two oceans for her!

I shall not lose courage, my love, she spoke to him silently. Not now that I am sure. Wait for me — just a little longer.

EPILOGUE

IN HER *Narrative of the Captivity of Mrs. Johnson* Susanna Johnson tells of the long journey from Montreal to Charlestown, New Hampshire. After months of wearisome delay in Quebec, the Johnsons, with many other prisoners of war, boarded a small sailing vessel which took four weeks to cross the Atlantic to Plymouth, England. There they waited until they could find passage on an English ship for the return voyage to America. It was with great thanksgiving that the family at last reached New York harbor and began the slow trip overland to the beloved Connecticut River valley.

A year later, a captive redeemed from the Indian village of St. Francis brought home with him Sylvanus, a wild young savage who could brandish a tomahawk and bend a bow but could not understand a word of English. Another prisoner, redeemed from Montreal, brought back little Susanna, a fine-mannered and fashionable young lady who could speak nothing but French and could never forget her deep affection for the two kindly women she had left behind.

The conflict between the French and the English for supremacy in the New World ended in the surrender of Montreal and victory for the English colonists. Some time after the close of the war, Phineas Whitney graduated from Harvard College and began his ministry in a small town in Massachusetts, and there he and Miriam Willard were married.